KRISTA

by

CHARLES NUETZEL

WRITING AS "FRED MACDONALD"

The Borgo Press
An Imprint of Wildside Press

MMVII

SECOND EDITION

Contents

Introduction

This is a book about a young woman who lived in Germany back in the 1950s, and carries a bit of factual background offered up by my wife.

A little "historical" explanation:

Wars come and go, and they all bring their savaging elements that stay with the survivors. What does this have to do with the present book?

Well my wife is a product of the Second World War. She was a young girl born and raised in Prussia, now a part of Poland. She is German. This book probably would not exist except for that reality. Brigitte gave me the background and the sense of what Germany was like during this period. The Berlin Wall didn't alter her own lifestyle, but it was a very ugly symbol of a Germany split into East and West.

The story of *Krista* takes place during these early years, in the harsh aftermath of that savage time when Hitler and his gang of Nazi monsters had driven a cultured, advanced nation down the tubes into total destruction. The country was overcrowded, and was still rebuilding itself from the crumbling ruins brought on by the war.

For a young woman, survival was a tough business. And because of that, Krista had been forced to continue living in her mother's home, even after the woman's death. She wanted a place of her own, but couldn't afford one.

Then one night alone with her stepfather, Krista was taught the brutal truth about life, men, and sex. Now no longer a virgin, she was forced to survive on her own, even if that meant using her body like a high-class whore in the flashy modeling business.

This is also a romantic story, almost a Cinderella tale of a girl who finds a way up through the nasty sink-hole around her, and into the arms of the one man who has the power to…

Oh, sure, another one of those romantic fantasies. But it was written for a publisher who was releasing original books that were supposed to have been written elsewhere in the world. Apparent translations.

Now that's a horrid professional confession, a look behind the scenes at the writer's life. If you want to make a living putting words to paper, you find a way to get them arranged in such a manner that pleases the publisher and those readers who will ultimately buy the book.

—CHARLES NUETZEL
Thousand Oaks, California
August 2006

Chapter One

This was the night when everything would change for Krista.

The apartment was older than most and the walls bare of pictures, yet there was a homey feel about the place. It was humming with light conversation and laughter, couples grouped off into three sets of *tête-à-tête*. Three people were at the radio, talking about the Berlin situation which was flaring up once more with the new Wall which the East Germans had just put up. Another group was around the slender middle-aged host, conversing about the living conditions and the overcrowded condition of the country. The third group was the smallest, a young girl and man, sitting and watching what was going on around them. They were holding small brandy glasses in their hands.

The party wasn't much different from other parties which are given during the year by the average German family. About ten people had been invited and were now in the process of sipping Weinbrand, rum and wine. It was the home of Karl Roher, a factory worker who had, after many years of effort, managed to reach the position of foreman. He had invited several couples from work and a couple from down the hall. Unlike many hosts, he had managed to consume a little too much of his favorite rum, and unlike many stepfathers, he was finding it hard to keep his eyes off his young stepdaughter, Krista Gustav.

Krista was sitting with her date, awkwardly aware of her stepfather's glances. She was a small girl with a full, voluptuous figure for her age. Her brownish blonde hair was long, flowing down several inches below her shoulders. The white cotton dress which made no attempt to accent her figure could not, at the same time, hide its attractive sensuality. The young man next to Krista was a clerk who worked with her at the office. He neither excited nor bored her. He was a convenience, nothing more or less: merely a companion for the party. It was the first time they had been together and it was obvious by the man's attitude that he was more than pleased by the event. For weeks he had attempted to entice Krista into letting him take her out. The conversation had lagged between them momentarily and they sat listening to the murmur of the conversations and music.

Krista had noticed the sidelong glances that Karl Roher had been giving her throughout the evening.

She wasn't too young to be able to read the very un-fatherly interest in his drunken dark eyes. It had been made painfully clear in the past months that he thought of her more as an unrelated woman living in the same apartment than as a stepdaughter. And his interest in women was strong enough so that she could easily imagine what dark thoughts were raging in his simple mind. His obvious awareness of her womanly figure had been a terrible strain on her mind and emotions. Every time he looked in her direction, Krista thought she would scream. If only her mother were still living, there wouldn't be any of this tension and interplay of glances. But she had been dead for five months; ever since then the relationship between Krista and her stepfather had become more and more awkward. She couldn't rid herself of the terrible feeling that some night—and not too far in the future—he would drink too much and the desires which were burning in his eyes would become animated with actions. How long she could continue to live under these conditions was impossible to tell. But there were very few options; if any. Apartments were difficult to get in Germany. Impossible for her.

"Pay some attention to me," Dieter Dobner exclaimed, grabbing hold of Krista's wrist. "You're supposed to be with me this evening."

Krista looked at the young man sitting next to her on the sofa. He was nice, though a little too forward for her taste. More Gisela Rettenbach's type. Dieter and Gisela had once been lovers some time ago, and because of that Krista hadn't felt too bad about allowing Dieter to be her date for this evening. It wasn't cutting into another girl's man.

For it had apparently been quite a love affair.

According to Gisela, at least.

"He's big and an artist in bed!" Gisela had told her.

Krista didn't think of him as physically attractive; but then she refused to think about physical relations between herself and a man. That was something for the future; right now she had enough problems without complicating them by getting romantically involved. Somehow she had to get out of her stepfather's home and find a place of her own before anything ugly happened.

"I'm sorry, Dieter, I was thinking."

"Well, think about me!" He leaned close and placed an affectionate kiss on her cheek.

Krista saw out of the corner of her eye the irritated look which her stepfather, Karl, gave Dieter. He was jealous. Why couldn't he think of her as a daughter, instead of just an unrelated young woman living in the same house with him? Karl was a stupid man! She hated him. If it weren't for Karl she would still be going to school and getting an education. But the moment her mother had died he had told her to get a job like any other girl, because he didn't have enough money to support her through school.

"You're no different than the other girls," he had said. "You can work, just like any other adult!" But that wasn't the full reason he had pulled her out of high school. He resented the possibility that the daughter of the woman he had married might become more educated than himself. He had never really liked the idea of having a stepdaughter. The other evening he had come into her bedroom while she was changing, and the way his eyes stared at her body had sent shivers down her nerves. It had scared Krista because she could read the thoughts which were running through his mind. If he'd been a little drunk he might have tried to do something with her.

If only apartments weren't so impossible to get, and so expensive! she thought bitterly. With her mere 260 DM a month, she couldn't begin to pay the price of even a room, if she could even get one. That was the trouble with Germany now. All the East Germans were running west, and crowding things so that nobody had anyplace to stay. It wasn't possible to put new apartments up fast enough to fill the demand. Young married couples lived with their parents and had no privacy. What chance did a single girl have without the 1,000 DM deposit required to get a halfway decent new apartment? Even then the first choice went to married couples with children. Someone like herself didn't even have a chance.

"Krista," Dieter said. "I've been talking to you for several minutes. What's wrong with you tonight?"

"I'm sorry. Maybe another brandy would help. I guess I'm just not in the party mood tonight."

In the next hours Krista managed to get more sociable with Dieter, enough so that he didn't have to force her out of a deep thinking mood. The party seemed to dwindle near Krista, the conversation blurring and the drinks of Weinbrand fading one into another. At last she found herself alone with Karl and Dieter.

"I guess I had better leave, too," Dieter said, standing and reaching for her. "Come downstairs with me?" he whispered.

There was no excitement at the idea of being alone with Dieter, but this offered a perfect chance to be away from her stepfather for a few more minutes. Krista couldn't help feeling that a scene was going to follow when Karl was alone with her, and she didn't know if she was up to it. Not that she was really afraid that he might actually get away with doing anything, but there was little doubt that he might try.

"Let's go," Krista told Dieter.

They stepped out of the apartment and went down the dark hallway. A few moments later they were downstairs, standing in the entranceway. Dieter tried to pull Krista into his arms, but she politely resisted. "Please—"

The expression of mixed emotions which worked Dieter's even features caused her to give in. The kiss was slow and lingering. She felt his tongue attempting to work past her teeth, and in a sudden moment of impulse she parted her lips and his kiss enter her mouth. It felt dizzily pleasant and caused a tremble to shudder through her.

They parted and she looked up into his eyes. Very few men had kissed her that way before, and she didn't actually know whether to be angry or delighted. The thought of her stepfather up in the apartment waiting for her caused Krista to say:

"Could you—could we go to a restaurant?"

"What?" Dieter's voice was thick with startled amazement. She could read in his eyes that he would much rather take her someplace more private. And that was the last place she wanted to go. She simply wasn't ready for that kind of relationship. Not with a man like Dieter Dobner. And that kind of intimacy she planned on saving for a man she loved. The first time had to be something beautiful and perfect. There was too much ugliness in living to make the most beautiful act become dirty, cheap and ugly.

"Please. I don't want to go up *there* right now!" Krista flashed her eyes up the stairs.

If Dieter read her real meaning, he was quiet. "Good. How about the *Weinstube zur Traube?* It's just a few blocks away, isn't it?"

"Yes, but—do you think we should have anything more to drink?" Krista asked, a little concerned about her already liquor affected brain.

"A carafe of port wine...it won't hurt."

Krista shrugged. It was better, the way she felt, to be with Dieter in a *Weinstube* than alone with her stepfather. She didn't think she could take another passionate stare from him this evening. Maybe by the time she got back he would be asleep. The longer she was out with Dieter the better chance she had of escaping any embarrassing clashes with the man.

"I'll go up and tell Karl." Krista turned and rushed up the steps and down the hall. Opening the door of the apartment, she called in: "I'm going to the *Weinstube* with Dieter."

Karl looked up from the glass of rum he had been drinking by himself. His thin face grew tighter. For a moment it looked as if he were about to argue with her, then he nodded. "Don't be too late. You have to clean up the place tomorrow!"

Krista joined Dieter a few seconds later and they walked out onto the street. The air was chilly and Krista mentally scolded herself for not having worn a coat. The dress she had put on for the evening wasn't made for outdoor wear. A shiver shook her and Dieter placed an arm around her shoulders.

"You should have brought something," he told her in a gentle voice.

They walked in silence, and the soft moonlight which showed through the crystal night seemed to lend a romantic air to the world. She could almost imagine herself with a lover, walking down the street, going no place of importance, merely being together. It was a nice dream and it ended when they arrived at the *Weinstube zur Traube*. It was a rather small *Weinstube* with an intimate atmosphere which was the pride of the district. The small tables for two were almost all taken, and they were led through the room to a dark corner.

"What will you have?" the waiter inquired.

"A small carafe of port wine," Dieter ordered. The man left.

In the far corner of the room someone played a zither, softly weaving a melody which Krista couldn't recognize. She had been here often—as often as her pocketbook could afford. It wasn't one of the most expensive places, but they still charged enough for food and drink to make it impossible as a daily or even weekly attraction. She was glad that Dieter had suggested it.

"Want a cigarette?"

She nodded. Dieter lighted one and placed it between her full red lips.

"You have beautiful lips."

"Thank you." She smiled shyly. Compliments had always embarrassed her.

They were silent for awhile, then Dieter broke it. "I wish it was because of me you wanted to come here."

"What does that mean?" She tensed.

"Oh, I have the feeling that you are—a little unhappy with your home relationship."

"What makes you think that?"

"Your stepfather has noticed you're an attractive

woman. I wouldn't want to be in his position." he laughed. "I bet it's not easy for a man to be around a woman like you."

Krista felt annoyed by the conversation, but decided not to say anything about it. The silence seemed to kill that topic. The small pitcher of wine, which Dieter had ordered, came and they began sipping the rich red port. It felt good in her stomach, and the effects slowly worked up through her body.

"It was a nice party Mr. Roher gave," Dieter commented conversationally.

"It was dull. You're just being nice."

"No—honestly, I enjoyed myself. I think the others did, too." He was thoughtful for a moment and then added: "I guess maybe it was because of you that I enjoyed myself."

"Hmmm. Thank you." She kept her eyes leveled at the small glass in her hands.

"I thought you'd never let me take you out. For weeks I've been saying to myself, 'What's wrong with you, Dieter?' I was beginning to think I'd lost my touch."

"You can't expect *all* the girls to fall at your feet."

"I don't. But a little bit. It's been a long time since I've been out with such a nice girl. Most of them are like Gisela."

"Do you think it's nice to talk about her?" Krista demanded tensely.

"I'm sorry. Just that she was the first that came to mind. I guess, because we both know her." He hesitated, then quickly added: "She's a nice girl."

It sounded lame, like an afterthought added on to cover up after his less complimentary comment about her.

They were silent for a moment, listening to the zither music. Krista was thinking about Gisela. The older girl had told her, one afternoon, that if she ever wanted to get out on her own, she could come live with her. Gisela had a place of her own, and it was the big mystery of the office as to how she had even managed to get an apartment. Some said that she had a man keeping her. A few of them thought she strung along several lovers. One person suggested that she was a prostitute in the evenings. Krista didn't think one way or the other about it. What Gisela did was her own business; how she managed to have an apartment and expensive clothes was her own secret and Krista wasn't one to take much stock in what others said. Still, she couldn't help wondering about the girl. Ever since the offer that Gisela had made, Krista had thought seriously about it, because it was the *only* offer— and the only possible way she could see to get away from her stepfather. But until things got seriously worse, Krista had decided it was far better to let them stay as they were than move in with a girl who had a questionable reputation.

"Gisela sure has a lot of beautiful clothes," Krista commented, hoping she might learn something about the girl.

"She *should* have."

"How's that?"

"Not for nice little girls to be told about. Just say that she has contacts—and knows the right people."

"Black market?" Krista offered, taking another sip of her drink.

"Heavens, no!" Dieter hesitated and then added:

"You were right, we shouldn't talk about other people."

"I'm sorry."

The conversation drifted then to office talk and then suddenly shifted to the personal.

Dieter had leaned closer to her and placed a hand on her arm. "You have the most beautiful dark blue eyes I've ever seen in a woman—they seem to have hidden passions and hidden desires, I'd give much to have the chance to give them full expression."

Krista felt a nervous reaction to his words, because she realized where they were leading. "Dieter, I don't want you to get the wrong idea about me. We hardly know each other."

Chapter Two

Karl Roher sat in the large olive green chair, staring blankly at the far wall.

It had been a good party, he thought, vaguely proud of himself. It wasn't often that he could afford a party, with his wife dead and his stepdaughter making so little money; but it was good to have one once in awhile. You got closer to your friends.

Life hadn't been easy for Karl. When he was a young boy his family had been poor and he just had finished normal school. By the age of fifteen he was working in Butchia as a *Laufbote.* During the war he had been in the service and then afterward had met Krista's mother. They had married when Krista was only about ten.

His thoughts drifted to his stepdaughter. It was hard living with such a beautiful young girl, and he wasn't the type of man who had ever wanted a child in the first place. He couldn't think of Krista as a child any more—she was a *woman,* and dressed like a woman. For weeks now he had been painfully aware of her sensual attractiveness. The evening when he had accidentally stepped into her room while she was changing had been plaguing his mind ever since. Her body was full and youthful. The large ripe swell of her breasts had been almost too inviting for his self control. It had been a long time since he'd had a woman—a very long time. And his taste for a female hadn't lessened at forty-five, but seemed to have grown *greater*. Krista's mother had been a good bed partner. She had known how to please a man and had been very passionate. Memory of her passion tormented Karl every night when he lay in bed, and his thoughts would turn to Krista and wonder if she were like her mother. And she was so close. So tempting. It was hell living like this. Especially since his wife was gone.

That woman, Karl groused, had been one bitchy whore in bed.

The way she'd grab at his groin, fondling him until he was hard and then use her lips, voluptuously tugging, kissing, and enveloping him within the confines of her mouth, the moisture of her tongue driving him to peaks of ecstatic pleasure was too much to remember. Every nerve in him wanted to experience that thrilling sensation.

How he craved the gripping passion of a woman's love-lips churning about his erected shaft, sending needles of pleasure through every nerve of his body.

Krista's mother had been passionately hot and admitted many times how wonderful he was.

There wasn't much that this woman would do, either, he remembered with a shiver of desire. Even anal intercourse, her fanny sticking up in the air, wiggling hotly, insistently begging him to enter its depths.

And the sounds she'd make at such times, like an animal, lusting, sobs and moans of pleasure.

Krista looked a lot like her mother and it was difficult at times to keep from grabbing her. After all, it wouldn't be incest since they were not related blood wise. He knew other men who had actually married their stepdaughters.

Karl cursed to himself, wanting to forget how Krista's mother had been; wanting to ignore the erotic beauty of this young woman sharing the same apartment—a body he could look at, want, but not touch. A body he couldn't keep his eyes off; or his mind lusting for.

It was a temptation, having her so near. After all it wasn't really unheard of to have relations with a stepdaughter.

Krista of the lovely hair and the full breasts. Her body was something from a movie screen. She could have been in pictures, as far as her beauty was concerned. In fact, he realized, she was a stunning woman, ripe for the taking. And how easy. Where could she go? How could she escape his demands? All he had to do was take her.

She could be his to have and enjoy and feast upon; to love like he had loved her mother.

Karl had known girls like her many times in the past, and this intimate knowledge helped to build the natural animal desires in him. The fogginess of his brain seemed to concentrate on Krista's image.

Maybe he should make his move—soon than later. Why wait?

Chapter Three

"It was a lovely evening," Krista told Dieter as they came to a stop before the apartment house where she lived. "It was so nice of you to take me to the Weinstube." The wine had drilled all reserve from her mind. She was standing very close to the man, unaware of the burning fires in his eyes. When his arms went around her, she melted willingly against his body.

They kissed for a moment and then she struggled away.

"Can't we go someplace together?" he pleaded.

"No, Dieter. I told you," she managed to say firmly.

The man sighed, then asked: "You'll let me take you out next Friday?"

"We can talk about that at work." She patted him on the cheek and turned, saying goodnight, and then going into the building. A couple of minutes later she opened the door to the apartment and stepped in. Her stepfather was sleeping in the large chair and she tiptoed through the room and went down the short hallway to her own bedroom, closing the door behind her.

Krista realized she should wake Karl, but something held her back. Instead, she started getting undressed. As she slipped out of her panties, she moved to the mirror on the closet door and looked at herself.

She had an attractive figure. It would have been good for modeling. Her breasts were high and full, the rosy centers pert and firm. The narrowness of her waist was just right for the rounded swell of her hips. Maybe her breasts were a little too large for a fashion model, she didn't know—but there were ways to take care of that.

Krista smiled at herself.

"I wonder what it might be like to be in love," she mused to herself. "Dieter is a lot nicer than I thought!"

Maybe love was a fantasy; not a reality in the real world. Maybe people just found an attractive partner they enjoyed being with. Was that all there was to it? Dieter was certainly nice. But, from what she knew of his reputation with the ladies, it seemed likely he might not be interesting in any real commitment. A one night stand was not what Krista considered possible with any man. She was determined to have a lover who respected her, who cared about her as a person, and whom she desired and cared about and loved, if possible. It had to be perfect. Not some cheap little quickie. No fast thrill. Nothing dirty. Something beautiful and lovely and perfect! Otherwise, what was the purpose, the meaning, or the reason for keeping oneself for that special person?

Krista shook her head, clearing such annoying thoughts away. This wasn't the time to be dealing with such concerns. Not after such a lovely time.

Yes. Dieter was nice.

She felt happy and content, because everything had worked out even better than she had hoped. Dieter had been asked to the party merely to fill out the couples, so that she would have someone to keep her company. But it had turned out to be a good thing.

Maybe he would be a nice guy to get to know. Maybe they would fall in love and get married. That would be one way out of her stepfather's home. Krista wondered why she hadn't thought about that before. Fall in love with a man. Or, even, it might be possible to merely let a man fall in love with her. All she would have to do would be to cook for him, take care of his apartment—if he wasn't living with his parents and had a place of his own. So she would have to let him make love to her—maybe that would be nice. She enjoyed being kissed and held by a man. And anyway that was just a normal part of life. It would be an escape.

But only escape.

It didn't fit with her other needs, her other longings for true love, a mutual feeling of oneness with a lover, a soul mate, perhaps.

Yes, that would be nice. That would be wonderful. That would be perfect!

That was a nice dream, but Krista knew that Dieter wasn't the marrying type. And she didn't know any men whom she would consider marrying. Things weren't that desperate—yet.

So that left her in limbo. In a dream-state, a fantasy world, in which reality had no place. But when reality took control of her thoughts, the lingering doubts came in, sucking away at the dreams until all that was left was harsh, cruel facts, with their horrid limitations. In another world, another place, even another nation, she might have a better chance at happiness, at that dream place, which American movies always presented on the screen. Fantasy. Make believe! Harsh reality was that you found somebody you could live with and you made the best deal you could. Nothing more.

Damn, I won't buy that. I won't give in. I won't let the world crush me! she thought.

But what could she do? Just live here with her stepfather and hope for the best—keeping him at arms distance! Avoiding the obvious. Cleaning up after him, doing the laundry, fixing meals, being a made, everything short of a wife. And for what? A room. Shared expenses.

It was better than living on the street!

She heard movement in the other room, then footsteps which grew louder.

Suddenly the door shoved violently open and Karl Rohm was standing there, drunk, staring blearily at her. Krista didn't have time to get any covering over her body. She stood there, terrified.

"Karl!" she cried angrily, trying to keep the fear from her voice "Get out!"

"You're beautiful, Krista.... A *woman*...You are...so...like your...mother. And...she was.... So passionate!" He staggered forward, cursing when he hit the bed and almost fell. "Don't be afraid."

"Get out of here! You're drunk!"

"I don't...*care!*" he snarled, moving toward her. "I've wanted you...for a long time. I've wanted you...it'll be beautiful...I promise!"

The world spun, shattered, closed in on her like

a horrid vice. She tried to tell her feet to run, to rush her bodily past the man standing there like a horrid monstrous wall.

The very thing which she had been afraid might happen someday was taking place right then. Krista felt her lungs choke, her body go cold as a chill rushed down it. Her hands tried to cover over her nakedness, but it was useless. "Karl—don't do anything—"

She didn't get a chance to finish, because the man leaped forward, his hands tangling with her arms.

"Krista! Krista!" he cried, attempting to crush his lips to hers. "Let me love you!"

"Karl!"

His hands were pawing at her breasts, and crushing around her, and sliding down between her legs. They seemed to be everywhere at once.

Terror caused her mind to go momentarily blank. It felt as if she were in a dark churning pit which closed in around her. She struggled, but from afar. She desperately attempted to hold off the drunken man, while at the same time finding it impossible to accept that it was happening.

Previously, thinking that Karl Roher might try anything to her had been only a childish fear. Not reality.

Now, abruptly faced with his sudden attack, she found herself trapped in a terrible nightmare, from which she could not escape.

All at once the bed hit her back and she felt the man lunge down against her. All emotion froze with the awareness that it was impossible to stop him, that he was much too powerful for her to struggle free. And she relaxed momentarily in defeat. But as his lips touched her, his tongue attempting to move past her teeth, panic gave her strength and she squirmed frantically. Her knees attempted to reach the point between his legs, but it was useless. His body had her clamped against the bed, and the weight was too much for her to overcome.

"Karl! Karl!" she cried, as his hands forced her arms down and pinned them to her sides. "Please!"

He ignored her. In his state of drunkenness she doubted that he even heard her pleas; she doubted he was even aware of her struggles.

His lips attempted to reach hers, but she kept moving her head to the side, avoiding contact. Finally he gave up with a curse and buried his mouth in her shoulder.

What was he doing? her mind screamed.

She felt helpless and weak, unable to combat the strength of the man's brutal strength forcing his animal desires on her.

All at once Krista realized she had waited too long to move away from Karl. If only she had gone with Dieter; that would have been far better than this horrid reality.

She tried to struggle away, but the more she moved, the wilder his kisses became, almost sucking on her flesh.

"Please!" she moaned, but he ignored her.

His right hand brutally cupped one of her breasts while the other held her firmly pinned to the bed.

Krista was aware of the hardness of his manhood pressing through the cloth at her groin.

God, he's going to rape me! her mind screamed

in terror. This was the hard real nightmare she had feared would happen if she waited to long.

She had waited too long!

Sensation stabbed through her as she felt his tongue touch voluptuously on her throat. A disgusting sickness that snapped at every nerve.

He seemed to be devouring her.

Then suddenly she felt him ripping at her flesh with cruel hands. His lips covered over one breast and sucked the nipple in deep, biting down with his teeth.

She screamed, but he slapped her face real hard and continued to work from one breast to the other.

One of his hands slipped down between them and tore at his pants.

Suddenly she felt something hard and fleshy pressing against her groin and panic set in.

He's going to! she sobbed deep inside her mind in frantic horror.

"Please...please! Don't! Please, Karl...don't!"

Then his hard erection started rubbing against her and she struggled hopelessly again. Every movement she made seemed to drive him into more passionate actions. Now he was holding her shoulders down with both hands, leaning over her like some savage beast.

His grunts and moans disgusted Krista.

Then suddenly she felt his hard shaft penetrate deeply into her and terrible pain erupted through her whole body like a knife had been slashed through naked flesh.

Sanity narrowed, blackness closed in on it, and only mad fury, terror, reached in around her consciousness.

Krista found herself suddenly trapped inside her mind, unable to move, unable to fight him any more, realizing it wouldn't do any good, now. Now it was too late. He had already ruined her body.

She would have to wait until he had finished his carnal rage. She would have to suffer through an endless flow of torture, of painful emotional horror, of harsh realization that her life had been shattered, crushed, destroyed beyond repair. There could be no turning back, no recovery. An ax had slashed down across her living experience and there was only the past fantasy and the cruel present reality and what was left of an uncertain future.

A disgusted moan of sickness filled her throat; she heard the sobbing and recognized it as her own.

Why this? Why this? Why did it have to happen this way? She had wanted to save herself for a lover. The first time it had to be beautiful and wonderful!

Pain kept stabbing through her. It was too late to ever find the perfection of love on her first relation with a man. It was over and finished. The purity of her body had been destroyed. She had been invaded and destroyed by a drunken man who could only think of his own selfish passions and degenerate desires. It was over and could never be taken back. Finished.

She lay in the bed of shame and disgust as the man moved savagely on her, until he had finally completed his lecherous act and sluggishly left her. But the pain and the disgust and sickness didn't leave with the man. It stayed, and suddenly she felt herself cramping up, doubled in agony as her guts erupted violently, as her whole insides ripped from her.

Sickness convulsed away and she lay back, dazed and unable to believe that it had happened. Unable to believe that this *could* happen. It was something you read about in the papers, something that happened to other people. It was a fantasy which didn't touch *you* only the dream world you read about.

Blackness settled over Krista for a long time— she didn't know how long. But it lay blanketed over her mind until suddenly she was sitting up in bed screaming, uncontrollably screaming out her horror,

Later, much later, when numb control finally ebbed through her mind like an icy hand, dulling all emotions, she got off the bed, grabbed her clothing and dressed, It took only a few minutes to get a few clothes packed, then she stepped from the room. Karl Roher wasn't anywhere to be seen, and she was glad. At that moment he wouldn't have been too hard to kill if he was unconscious and unable to defend himself.

Quietly, without any thought as to where she was going, she checked through her purse, counted the 30 DM which were in it, and then moved out of the apartment forever.

Chapter Four

Gisela Rettenbach bathed in the caresses of the man with a wild hunger, the kind which had plagued her since her early teen years.

"Oh, it feels great!" she moaned, responding to the first naked touch of him against her. She squirmed against the man, moaning I delight. "I love that!"

The man cupped her ample breasts and started to tongue them deliciously, moving from one to the other.

She fondled and squeezed his buttocks in rhythm with their movements. She was in an ever expanding well of joy, being feasted on like that, hungrily devoured, longing for the deep penetration soon to unit their bodies into one surging mass of pleasure.

They had started the usual way, getting undressed and then kissing deeply upon one another's tongue, while her hips rubbed against his groin, making it respond to the raw, blatant stimulation. She captured him between her thighs, gently twisting and rocking, tugging and pulling on its length. Then all at once they were on the bed, her head between his legs.

30

Gisela felt sudden pleasure rip through her as the man's shaft started to entered her.

Greedily her hips surged up, voluptuously thrilling to the feel of a man tucked so deeply within her.

Her hands embraced his head, pulling it down to her lips. The feel of his tongue as it entered her mouth sent a wild erotic orgasm through her. She sucked violently on his tongue, drawing it deeply into her mouth as she had upon his beautifully hard erection.

The moment of pleasure was so intense that she trembled like a leaf up against him.

He rode with the punches, slowly entering and withdrawing in a torturous tempo that drove her crazy with pleasure.

"Oh, you're good!" she moaned, feeling the wonderful sensation of him surging in and out of her. And suddenly she was aware of the rebuilding of another wave of overwhelming pleasure.

Heinz was such a good lover, her mind sobbed in joy. His skill and experience matched hers. Of all her lovers she found him most satisfying.

"Come, come, on and on!" she sobbed.

"Shut up and enjoy yourself," he demanded tensely. "I can't keep this up much longer...if you...don't take it easy!"

"Oh, do it!" she pleaded.

His rhythm changed and suddenly she felt sure this would be the best she had had for weeks.

Her whole guts felt as if they were going to erupt. Then suddenly he plunged deep, filling her total ecstasy.

Her whole body curled in on itself as she experienced her own orgasm like a multiple series of ever building waves that climaxed so wildly that she screamed out in the pleasure of it, falling back on the bed all but exhausted out of her mind.

Yet he was still wildly alive.

"Oh, Heinz, not again!" she moaned in delight.

She gripped him with her legs holding his hips in place.

"Oh, you are wonderful!" This time it was a fast, almost savage jerking of their bodies. She felt his hands grip around her breasts, squeezing and she squeezed back on the muscular buttocks that was snapping up and down like hammers.

Gisela had never had more than one other lover who could pop a second orgasm into her body without leaving her.

Heinz was the best.

"Oh, love," she moaned, out of her head with joy.

A sound burst from his mannish lips that told her more than any words might have, that he was reaching the end of his rope.

Then she felt him lunge down, a plunging lunge that sent her deep into a beautiful voluptuous series of sensations that threatened to devour all consciousness.

Suddenly the peak of ecstasy waved over her total being, and she heard her own voice scream out into the darkness of the small bedroom. Then the man fell away and she floated on the sea of exhaustion which finally washed her onto the shore of half sleep. In that state her mind wandered back over her life—a life that hadn't been easy. She had struggled for a bare existence after the war, getting her room and board through the use of her body. It had been the only way to survive, and she had used it to the best of her ability. There were a lot of American GI's ready to pay good money for her body, and she had managed to scrape through those torn years which were the bitter aftermath of national defeat. And those years had given her the contacts which finally placed her in a rather good apartment, with a fairly high salary for what little she was trained to do. It wasn't a bad life which she had chopped out for herself; it provided her basic needs, and more luxuries than a girl in her position could otherwise afford. She was just glad that those years of selling herself like a prostitute were over. Things had changed since then, and she had got along with "lovers"—like Heinz—who gave costly gifts for her attentions. And more than that, gave her so much sexual pleasure that sometimes she felt over-whelmed with utter magic of their unions.

Dimly she heard soft knocking on the front door. At first it was impossible to recognize it for what it was. Then the huge brute of a man next to her nudged Gisela.

"Who's that? Who'd be wanting to see you at this hour of the morning?" His voice was heavy with anger.

"Nobody!" Gisela cried, sitting up, her slender body naked to the man's stare. She felt his hand move to her shapely breasts, lightly touching one erect nipple.

"Don't!" she ordered, irritated.

"Ignore it!" he cursed, forcing her backward onto the bed, his lips seeking hers. She struggled with him; when his hands caressed her breasts, she gave in. The warmth and pleasure which his touch built in her tall form caused Gisela to moan softly.

The knocking repeated, louder this time. Both of them froze, "Honestly, I don't know who it could be," Gisela whispered, defensively.

"Ignore it!" Heinz's hand cupped one breast, sending pleasure stabbing through her slender form.

A soft voice called: "Gisela! Gisela, are you there?" The knocking became very loud; now someone was pounding on the door.

The voice sounded familiar, but she couldn't place it. She forcefully pushed the man away, then sighed. "I'd better go see who it is."

"It'll go away, if you just—"

"No. I'd better find out. The neighbors will be angry at the noise. I'll be right back!"

Gisela slipped away and reached for her night robe, pulling it around her body and tying it. She stepped across the living room to the front door. "Who is it?" she demanded softly.

"Krista Gustav."

For a moment her mind was simply blank with amazement. Krista was one of the girls who worked with her at the office. They had been quite friendly but nothing more.

What was she doing here? Gisela wondered.

"What do you want?"

"Can I come in?"

She hesitated, unsure of what to do. The man in the bedroom wouldn't like the idea of another woman coming in at the middle of their bedroom activity. But she couldn't turn the girl away without some reason.

"Why are you here?"

"You *said* I could come here if I ever needed a

34

place to stay." The voice was desperate and afraid, small and lost.

Gisela decided, and opened the door.

* * * * * * *

The room was dark as Krista stepped into the apartment. Gisela turned on a light and then walked across the room to close a door which led into her bedroom. The woman was brisk and seemed nervous. She turned, staring in confusion at Krista.

"I'm sorry, Gisela!" Krista's voice choked tightly in her throat. Suddenly the tears which she had been holding back flooded into her eyes. Sobs racked her chest, and suddenly she was being held by the other girl.

'What's wrong? What's wrong?" Gisela demanded, concerned. She patted Krista's hand. "It's not that bad. It can't be. What happened?"

"I left Karl. I don't have any place to stay—I don't know what to do. I walked for a long time, I don't know how long. But I didn't know what to do! I could have gone to a hotel, but...but I didn't want to be alone tonight. I remembered...remembered what you said several times to me...that if I ever wanted to have a place...I know it's without warning, but I...."

Krista broke down again. The desperation, the wanting to tell someone what had happened, and knowing this was the last thing she *could* do, crushed her emotions which had already been stripped raw.

Gisela led her to a sofa and stood over her without saying anything. Then she moved away and disappeared.

Krista heard voices, but couldn't understand at first where they were coming from. Then she realized there was conversation going on in the bedroom, and it hit her.

What had she done?

It hadn't occurred to her that Gisela might have a man with her. That was one thing she hadn't planned on. What could she do? Impulse caused her to stand and start for the door.

"Krista!" Gisela cried, rushing across the room toward her. "Where are you going?"

"I...I didn't know..." she sobbed in anguish.

"Don't be silly. He was leaving, anyway. He understands. Don't be silly!"

Gisela grabbed hold of Krista's shoulder and pulled her away from the door, leading her back to the sofa. "You just stay right here! Everything will be all right." Gisela paused and then looked thoughtfully down at Krista. "Could you use a drink? You look like it might do you some good!"

Krista started to shake her head, then reconsidered. Maybe a drink *would* help. Maybe it would help to wash away that terrible memory of what had happened that night. Her body ached from Karl Roher's brutal attack; her mind was still in a state of emotional shock. It just didn't seem possible that this was happening to her. It couldn't be happening—yet she knew it was reality. Cold, terrible reality.

She could still feel the shape of his ugly male thing assaulting her body, again and again shoving itself into her womanhood like some perverse kind of hard, stiff snake.

How she had wanted the first time to be beautiful.

But instead he had taken her legs, parted them, brutally thrust into her, taking away everything that might have been given to the man she would someday marry.

Krista had heard stories about how it should be with a woman. Some of her girl friends had, like Gisela, told of the beautiful experience sex was supposed to be.

Would she ever have that kind of experience? Krista wondered in anguish.

A shudder rushed down her spine as she remembered stories of how women had almost been unconscious with pleasure while experiencing sex with a lover.

Krista feared it would be impossible for her to ever enjoy a sexual act after what Karl had done.

Then her mind froze on that thought. How many other young girls had been raped and finally adjusted to sexual relations with other men? Surely it might be possible for her.

Oh, God, she hated that man! Krista inwardly sobbed.

Gisela handed her a glass with brandy in it. "Here, take this. It'll help. I'll be back,"

Gisela disappeared into the bedroom. There was muffled conversation, then she returned with a man following her.

"You do understand, Heinz?"

The man grunted, looked at Krista, then shrugged. "I'll talk to you tomorrow?"

"Sure, sure. Thanks a lot. You're wonderful."

Gisela slipped her arms around the man and

they kissed briefly at the door. Then he was gone. The girl turned and moved over to Krista. "Come on, drink up. Do what Gisela tells you." The woman's voice was strong and forceful, but gentle and understanding. "Whatever it was—you don't have to tell me—it must have been something pretty bad."

"Oh, Gisela, you don't know how—how much—thanks!"

Krista gulped the brandy, which burned in her throat. She coughed. After a long silence she looked up at Gisela. "I should...you have a right to know what happened, why I came here. I know I didn't have the right to—"

"Don't be silly! I've felt close to you. We can have a grand time together." Gisela brushed her blonde hair back and then looked tenderly down at Krista. "A man?"

"It was Karl...what I was afraid of..." She couldn't force more from her lips, but it was enough.

Gisela cursed. "That no-good bastard! *Das verflüchte Schwein!*" The woman's arms went around Krista, and she found herself sobbing again.

"Oh, it was horrible. He stuck that horrid thing in me and it was terrible! I couldn't get away and...."

"Don't talk about it!" Gisela soothed.

Some time later, though, the woman said: "Poor child. It should have been a beautiful experience with a nice lover."

Krista looked at Gisela, slowly shaking her head. "What man would look at me now?"

"Don't be silly, they don't know what's up. A

girl can tell them anything." Then quickly Gisela explained: "The first men I had after having been seduced almost against my will—they believed whatever I told them. Even now I'll play it that way if it is necessary. You can do anything to a guy and he'll believe you if you said it was the first time!"

Gisela continued to hold her, even closer, protectively, like a mother or older sister, making a safe zone, a place where nothing could hurt her. It was a long, long time before control returned and she allowed the other woman to lead her into the bedroom to find rest in exhausted sleep.

Chapter Five

The next morning seemed strange and alien to Krista. She couldn't emotionally accept what had happened the night before, even though it was impossible to deny its reality. The strange bed, the strange room.

And Gisela Rettenbach.

All day Krista moved in a daze. She ate little, and talked even less. The other woman was quietly understanding, ready to do anything for her during this time of need. She called a doctor friend of hers, who came over and examined Krista for any physical harm which Karl Roher's act might have caused. In the next days he visited Krista, then finally the visits faded out.

These days were a long horror for her, each blending into the next. Gisela had gone to Karl Roher's apartment and picked up Krista's things. The man hadn't asked any questions. and everything had gone smoothly

Gisela left for work in the mornings, usually returning by six in the evening. Several times she went out at night and returned late. But for the most part, during the first couple of weeks, she made it a point to be with Krista, or see to it that there was somebody to keep her company. Slowly the emotional and mental effects of what had happened to her began to lose their more intense power.

During this time, Gisela slowly managed to give Krista a different outlook about life and sex by telling of her own experiences.

Once in detail, Gisela told how she'd seduced a man, stripping in front of him, thrusting her hips out and saying how he really made her hot. "I wanted it, terribly. It can be so good once a girl understands her body. I've done a lot of things with a man and that night I wanted to do everything my mind might imagine," she told Krista as they sat on their bed. "You don't know what it is like until experiencing the real thing with a real man.

"Believe me, when you get a lover who knows how to do it right with you, all your attitudes about sex and men will change."

But Krista shook her head, remembering how terrible the night with Karl had been. "I don't think I'll ever be able to enjoy it."

"Look," Gisela scolded, leaning closer, "a girl has feelings between her legs that can only be released when a man's hard is placed there. You feel there, don't you? I know you do. What happened to you was terrible, but not the end of the world. It happens to a lot of us; and we get over it. Once you feel a man between your thighs, press that hard flesh, feel the hotness, you'll think different about the whole thing. Just like I did that time...the first one I really couldn't control myself. I couldn't wait to get his cock between my thighs and twist and tug on it until lie was frantically desperate."

Then she'd gone into details that had more or

less shocked Krista. Telling how they had stripped and pressed against one another until he was "rock hard."

The details that Gisela confessed to about how she moved against the man are hard actually created a strange and horridly perverse longing within Krista. She was jealous of the other woman's ability to be so intensely happy about such experiences. She wondered if it would ever be possible to want that kind of thing to ever happen to herself. She wanted to know such feelings, such joy, pleasure, and at the same time never wanted a man to come near her. The very idea of that revolted her on a conscious level. Yet a basic part of her reacted. That was strange, because she didn't want to feel anything.

"Oh, it is just wonderful being with a man who really cares, who is caring and skilled. Look, honey, just take it from mc that there is simply nothing in the world better."

And another time the woman told of going down on a man, and how much she enjoyed that, too. There didn't seem to be any limits to the woman's pleasure with a man, nor anything she wouldn't do with or to her lovers.

Krista hadn't known about such things. But over the days living with Gisela she learned all the by-ways of lovemaking, even to the detailed responses the girl experienced during anal intercourse.

Krista was certain about one thing: it would be difficult enough to ever give herself to a man and just about impossible to do such perverse things as this woman told her about.

Still the conversation did have a general effect

42

of slowly changing her attitude. Where in the beginning it had seemed impossible to ever consider sexual acts with a man, it became less and less difficult to accept after hearing the many versions of Gisela's sexual experiences over the days and nights when they would talk of such things.

Then one Saturday afternoon Gisela took Krista out to a movie and then to a *Gaststube* for some beer.

It was too early for any social activity. The place was decorated in the old-fashioned pre-war style, with heavy wooden tables and chairs.

They stayed only long enough to have a couple of beers. The owner, a Mr. Neu, was a huge fat man who came up to Gisela and joked about all the male friends she had chasing after her.

"I see you've picked up a friend. You should bring her here in the evening. The men would like her," he said, looking at Krista.

After the beer came they sat, saying little. Gisela finally started talking seriously to Krista, speaking in a low voice.

"I know this isn't really the time to be talking about such things, but since we're planning on being roommates, we might as well understand a few things." Gisela hesitated, then asked, "I guess you must know I have many things which my job at work could never pay for? I get such things from men."

Krista listened, but her mind wasn't really on what the other woman was saying. She just nodded at the right time.

"A girl can get a lot of things if she knows the right men and is willing to do certain things for them. You don't have to like the men, but you make them think you do. A man is a fool—he'll do anything for a woman. And after what happened to you, I guess you'd like to turn things around and get even with men. They are animals, and use women if they get the chance."

Gisela's last words caught Krista's full attention.

"What do you mean?" she asked, interested now.

"Well, men are *Schwein.* All they want of *women* is our bodies. And if a girl is willing to give her body to the right guys. she can have a lot of things. A very, very lot of nice wonderful things."

"That's prostitution!" Krista said with amazement, numbed and startled by the way she could even say the word, let alone seriously consider it. The idea had never occurred to her before. Yet she realized it might not be so bad—nothing could be *that* bad after what had happened to her.

"Not prostitution. Nothing as sordid as that, Krista. Just letting the right men have you—the men who will see to it that you get a few favors in return," Gisela told her. "Men you might actually enjoy being with. And you are always the one in control of the situation. That's a real power trip. Believe me! After the war I got along by using my body—it was the only way I could survive. And now it's the only way I'm able to get little things I want—by having the *right* lovers.

"Until you've had a real man give you a good one, it is impossible to know how great things can be.

"Why, the first man I ever blew—I never real-

KRISTA, BY CHARLES NUETZEL

ized how great it could be to kiss a man liked that. It sounded so terrible.

"He demanded I do it to him and the idea of what he would give in return forced me to keep him happy. I was being offered a one-room apartment to give him some joy.

"He stripped down his pants and suggested I get down on my knees before him. I hesitated, then reconsidered. It wouldn't kill me and it was impossible to get apartments then. As you well know.

"Well, I fell before him and he gripped my head, holding it in place

"I didn't know I would enjoy it so much. There is simply something wonderful about doing that to a man. I've loved it ever since. And men will give a girl a lot of good things just for doing something like that to them. It doesn't cost you any more than a little time and care. And it is so safe! You don't have a chance of getting pregnant that way. They are such suckers for a sexy woman that you can't miss. And with your body it would be a shame to be a fool. Most girls give it away for free. That is cheap. That, to me, is being dumb, and sluttish. The way I hand it out is smart. Not cheap! Nothing cheap or dirty, but something which seems respectable. Like with Heinz. He helps to get me a lot of things. He might help you, too, if you played up to him. I could have Heinz bring a friend along some evening."

Krista thought that over for a moment and then said: "Give me time. Wait until I've returned to work for a few days. Maybe I should start at the office again tomorrow. I feel a lot better now, and I can't just live off you all the time."

45

The conversation drifted after that, and they left when their drinks were finished. The next morning Krista returned to the dullness of office work. Everybody wanted to know what had been wrong, and she just told them it was a sickness. If they had learned the truth, they didn't say anything about it.

Dieter came up to her desk and wanted to know when he could take her out. "You weren't at your stepfather's place, and he wouldn't say anything about you. What happened?" He seemed concerned.

"Nothing. I just moved out. I couldn't stand it there. Then I became sick."

He merely nodded, then said: "If there's ever anything I can do for you, just let me know."

"Thanks."

"How about coming out with me sometime? I enjoyed myself very much that evening. I thought...maybe you enjoyed yourself, too."

"I did, but just give me time. I still don't feel too well," she told him, avoiding a direct answer. Krista didn't know if she could face being alone with a man. Even a nice one like Dieter.

In the next days the job began to drill on her nerves, and Krista realized it was because of the memory symbols it brought into focus. It reminded her of the months living with Karl Roher, of that horrible night with him. Every time she saw Dieter he was another harsh reminder.

Finally one evening Krista told Gisela how she felt about her job. "If only I could get out of it! Do something else. I don't want to be an office girl all my life."

"I *could* introduce you to some men, but what is it you want to do?"

46

"What could I do?"

They talked about it for a long time, and then Gisela happened to mention that Heinz knew a man in the fashion business: "With your figure, just a little changing here and there, with your hair—you could be very good in that field."

The idea excited Krista. Something like that could be profitable and interesting. "What would I have to do?"

They were sitting in the front room, sipping brandy. The evening was drifting away into morning by the time a plan of action had been outlined.

"You have to understand, Krista, that men want something for the favors they might do for you."

"I understand," she said meekly, depressed at the thought of letting a man have her body. Or even touching her.

"It's not like it was with you and Karl. It can be good, if you have a good lover. And you don't really have to enjoy it to make them *think* so. I can tell you what to do, and how to please a man. What he expects from a woman. Play it right and you'll be able to make your own way. I've just been waiting for you to open up on this. I can have Heinz bring this friend of his over and—how about tomorrow?"

Krista was reluctant, at first unsure of herself, but the thought of being introduced to a man who might get her into the modeling business finally overpowered all reluctance.

"I don't know..." was her careful remark.

"Come on, you can't live like this all your life. You have to start living and loving. What difference does it make, especially now, if you don't really think you'll enjoy *it* with a man? Maybe things will look different after you've tried it out. You have to face reality. Men have hard-ons all the time! I mean, you'd be surprised: they go around on three legs! Really! They are different from women. They need to get it off. They need to release themselves—they can't really control all that…it is a body function, like…well…peeing!" She giggled at that.

"Really?" Krista laughed in response.

"Really! One guy told me that he almost resented women, especially when he was a teenager. 'They tease you with their breasts all sticking out, and don't have any idea how hard a guy gets. It is like having a continual pain between your legs. You get the feeling the girls are saying: look but don't touch!' Men are walking around all day long thinking about being with a woman. Every women they see is a possible turn on for their hurting little men dangling down there, screaming in pain to be getting a bit of loving release! That little guy has no sense of morality, simply wants…no *needs*…to get his release, one way or another. A hard is painful ás hell! And it'll go for just about any woman who will service his needs. Take it in your hands, mouth or…body…and he'll be so delighted that if you play it right…well…you're in control of the situation and he's helpless. Poor guy! Give them what they so desperately want and they'll be delighted. And it is just as easy to take a rich guy into bed with you as it is some poor working class jerk without the hard cash to make it worth your time and energy. He doesn't have to know if you liked it or not. Fake it, if necessary. You have to face it that bluntly. If you don't give in to the right men you will be stuck— in more than one way!"

"Do you have to put *it* that way?" Krista objected, shuddering inwardly.

"Sex is sex. Believe me. After you've tried it a little while, you'll start responding. I know you're a normal woman. You've just been cooled off because of a terrible sexual experience. Don't let *it* ruin your life. And if you do hate men so much, why not just use them? Just let their hot cocks be serviced by your body and make them pay high for the right. Otherwise you're in for a very dull life. Men won't give a woman the time of day unless there's hope of a little screwing. One way or another, that's all men want. Some call it love, some are honest enough to call *it* nothing more than screwing. I learned my lesson a long time ago, why don't you realize I've been telling you the blunt truth?"

Krista shrugged her shoulders, defeated. There was no escaping Gisela's logic. If she wanted to get ahead in the world, it was necessary to let men come into the circle of her life. No matter how she might dislike it. The world was run by men; maybe there wasn't anything wrong in simply using her body to get ahead. What difference did it really make .Men were animals and beasts. All they wanted was to sleep with a girl. So, let them try—and pay the high price!

It was agreed that they would have the two men over the next evening, and all that night Krista found herself tossing and turning in bed with nightmares.

The erotic level of the dreams was frightening. During one she imagined a huge erected penis standing up in front of her, a voice saying, "Kiss it, kiss *it!*" Just as hands gripped her head, forcing her toward the huge male thing, she woke, sweating.

Yet there was a strange sense of excitement. She had made up her mind about doing something positive, instead of simply existing. It was just necessary to turn off her emotional reactions; to simply go through the motions, blanking everything out. That might be possible. Maybe.

If she wanted out of office work, and entrance into a rich field of modeling, then she might simply have to deal with the reality that men ruled the world and that she could learn to control some of them by using her body to get much desired favors. Nothing could be as horrid as what Karl had done to her; and in this case she could be the one in control. That idea was fascinating. Control was the key to everything in life. If you had the power in your hands, it made all the difference in the world.

Maybe that was the right way to get ahead. Maybe Gisela was right.

Maybe was probably the wrong word.

Krista made herself say it in her mind: *This was the fast way out of the gutter. And into modeling.*

She had mental images of parading before a group of rich women, showing off an original dress design, being applauded and made over as the world's leading fashion model. It was an image to be desired and she began believing it would be worth any price to gain such fame.

The more Krista thought about it, the more excited she became.

The next morning, exhausted from lack of sleep, she had to force herself to get up, shower and dress. All that day Krista kept dreaming about herself as a world-famous fashion model, with lovers the world around seeking her attention. It was in that excited state that she returned home with Gisela and put on the finishing touches of new makeup. She felt like a different girl—a woman, whose name was Krista Gustav, but who was in another body. All her life she'd been a little afraid to show how good her figure was. Now it showed off sensationally in the raw beauty of womanhood, without being either cheap or crude. It had a high-class, fashionable appearance. The dress, which revealingly accented her large breasts, had made her feel a little embarrassed when she first put it on. Now, with the facial makeup, *it* seemed as natural as breathing.

Krista's hair had been pulled up onto her head in an *Einschlagrolle,* much in the fashion of the Japanese woman, though simpler, baring her neck and delicately shaped ears. Gisela had tried earrings and then decided they didn't look good on Krista. Her already full lips had been marked much larger than she had ever made them, giving a voluptuousness which seemed to be an open offering to a man. Blue shadow and dark lines surrounded her eyes, enlarging their shape and giving an innocent expression which was in contrast to the rest of her face. Gisela had drawn her eyebrows high and arching, thicker than she would have thought correct. Instead it gave that final touch which created an image of a woman who has lived, but managed to retain her innocent expression and outlook.

"You should bleach your hair soon. That's what you need; then it will be perfect. But it's better to have something in reserve. You can have that added plus on your second meeting with Werner Pawlík."

Krista let her eyes drop to the front of the blue

dress which Gisela had found for her. It was far more daring and revealing than she normally would have had the courage to wear. But that was part of the trap which Gisela was setting. All part of the female mantrap which was sure to capture Krista some rewards.

Gisela looked at her wrist watch, then straightened up. "They'll be here in a little while. You want something to drink before they get here?"

Krista jumped at the idea. She needed something to give her courage to face the first moments with the men. She felt like a child on her first date, unable to handle the situation. And in a way this was almost true. This was the first date she'd accepted with the express idea of letting a man have his way.

She sat there gazing at herself and finding it amazing that so much could have happened so soon. Karl Roher's forced seduction seemed far away, and didn't have too much power over her any more. The doctor had told Krista that her mind would cover over the emotional scar. He'd said that chances were, the shock of the event would keep it numbed for a long, long time—and when it did once more come into full focus in her emotions, she would have grown enough that it wouldn't affect her any more.

"You're coming a long way, Krista," she told herself, smiling. "You're quite beautiful. I never knew you were so beautiful. With your looks and a willingness to please men, there's no telling how far you might go."

Krista sat there thinking about that, wondering exactly where her life would lead her. No thoughts of the morality of what she was doing entered her mind, for too much had happened to let her even accept morality as a part of her life. Suddenly she felt happy, released from all concern and worry. Her mind was abruptly excited about the evening ahead. Maybe it might be fun, getting even with men, using them, using her body to get things from them. A man wanted to get a woman into bed, and he would pay a lot of money to get her there. He would do almost anything to obtain the object of his desire.

Sitting in front of the mirror, looking at herself, Krista made up her mind that she was going to use everything in her power to get whatever she could from men; use her God-given body and beauty to obtain exactly what she wanted—freedom, money, a life of ease. One thought came to plague that contented mood. Exactly how far would she go? Prostitution? And she didn't know.

Gisela returned to the bedroom and handed her a half-filled brandy glass. Krista took it and downed most of the liquor in one swallow.

"Hold on, girl! You'll have a lot of drinking to do this evening, and you don't want to get too much out of hand." Gisela patted her cheek affectionately. "Just remember; be charming, don't babble too much. Get the man talking about himself, and listen. Add the right words at the right time, make the right comment. Be attentive and affectionate when it is proper to be so, but don't be forward. Let him take the lead, but make sure he knows that he'll be welcomed with open arms. When he makes a direct pass, hesitate just a little, then try to make him think he is overpowering you with his bloody little man. If he wants to do something this evening, be sure you have the upper hand. If you don't, stall him off, making him think that the next time he sees you he'll probably get what he wants. The fine line between being cheap and easy, or merely a mature woman who will willingly enter into a relationship with a man because it is only natural and normal, is hard to find. You have to walk easy and be sure you are leading, while at the same time making him think that *he's* the one who's doing the leading. There's always your body. You will have that one thing—that he'll desire *always*—to use. Save it for the most important moment. Play it right, and you'll have him eating anything you hand out."

Gisela stepped back, then said: "Stand—let me see you."

Krista stood and turned slowly around. The flaring skirt twisted slightly with the action of her body.

"You'll do fine! Just—"

There was a knocking on the front door. Gisela broke off, smiled knowingly and warmly at Krista, then gracefully moved from the room.

Krista listened as the other woman opened the front door and ushered the two men in. Then, taking a deep breath to hold down the nervousness which was suddenly grinding at her stomach, Krista finished the rest of the brandy and stepped out into the living room.

Chapter Six

They had been out dancing and drinking for over three hours before the heavyset Werner Pawlík made his first pass. He was a gross man, and had little physical attraction for Krista. She doubted that he could get many women purely on his animal appeal. He had small eyes, and his mouth was thick lipped and weak looking. They were dancing when he brushed his lips against her neck. "You're a beautiful woman, Krista. The most beautiful I've met for a long time."

"Well, thank you. But with all the girls in your profession, surely you meet some who are—"

"None!" he whispered, pressing her closer, moving his hips in rhythm with the music. The soft lighting in the club was dark enough to hide any such intimate actions, so Krista didn't feel too nervous.

By now the drinks they had consumed during the evening had worked a light effect over her body, and she didn't care much about anything. Luckily, because the man was almost repulsive to her. When she had seen him in Gisela's apartment earlier. Krista had felt her stomach clamp tightly against her spine. Then she had forced a smile and managed to hide the real feelings that were icing in the back of her mind. When they had left to go barhopping, she had determined to get herself good and high. It seemed as if she were spinning through a dream world which had little reality.

"Where has Gisela been keeping you?" Werner questioned as they started to move from the dance floor.

"I've been around, but in different circles until now, that's all," Krista told him lightly. He helped Krista into her seat and then settled in the next one. His hand reached under the table and Krista felt the fingers move along her thigh.

"We could have a lot of fun together, if we were someplace else." The fingers slipped under her dress, and Krista tensed.

Forcing a smile, she said: "You're a nice guy. Would you really think much of me if I should—?"

He didn't let her finish the sentence. "Don't be childish. A woman like you.... I wouldn't think of doing anything that wasn't respectable. It's just that I thought it would be so much more fun to be alone together. Maybe we could slip off someplace."

Just then Gisela and Heinz joined them. "Are you two having fun?" Heinz asked, hardly looking at them.

"Fun enough," Werner said laughingly. "I've been trying to get this young lady to leave with me, but she's inclined to stay."

"That's not true," Krista explained hurriedly. "I just said that, well, I wanted to make sure we understood each other."

Gisela gave her a sharp look. "Why don't the two of you run along? We'd sorta like to be alone, ourselves."

"Then it's settled," Werner declared, turning to Krista. "I'm a little tired of dancing, so let's maybe take a ride."

The way he said the words told Krista all too clearly that he wasn't suggesting a ride in a car, but a ride in the bed. A nervous flutter rushed down her spine as they stood and said goodnight to the other two. When they were outside, Werner suggested that they go up to his place for a drink.

This was the moment which both of them had been waiting for all evening—each with different motives, different emotional responses, and different ends in mind.

The nervousness clamped once more inside Krista, then she remembered how it was working at the office, with its endless reminders of what her life had been like with Karl Roher. This was a possible escape. If she failed here, she would at least learn what not to do.

"Okay. Let's go," Krista managed to say, letting the man take her arm in his. They walked to where he had parked his car.

It was late; even the moon had dropped beyond the horizon. The drive to his apartment took just a little over fifteen minutes. When they stepped into the living room, he quickly turned on the radio and picked a music station. In moments he had mixed what he called "martinis." She had never had one, and the first sip startled her.

"I acquired a taste for them through some American and English friends of mine," Werner told her, sitting down beside Krista on the gray sofa. "They're strong, but they have a nice taste to them.

I've found the English gins much better than the American. They have a much smoother taste."

Krista was hardly listening. She was looking at the living room with a sense of inner amazement. In magazines she had seen such places, and in the movies. But never in her life had Krista been in such luxury. Surely it must cost at least 300 DM a month. There was a small home bar in the far corner, and what looked like high-fidelity speakers on the wall opposite them. All the furnishings were off-white, with black masking. The lush wall-to-wall carpeting was like nothing she had ever seen.

"You have a very nice place," she managed to say.

"I've arranged to get a few things I want." Werner hesitated, then went on: "Heinz tells me you are interested in modeling."

Krista felt a sharp surprise at his words. All evening she had been trying somehow to bring the subject up, but it hadn't been possible. "I would like to get into such a line," she answered carefully.

"You sure do have the figure for it. A little polish and you could become very popular. Haven't you had any training?"

"None, I'm afraid."

"That doesn't matter much. We could take care of that in a short time." Werner took another swallow from his drink and then shrugged. "Enough of that tonight. There are many more interesting things to talk about, besides work. Don't you agree?"

Krista nodded and then sipped her cocktail. It felt very strong; with each sip she took, a light dizziness clamped tighter around her forehead.

The conversation drifted and then circled around

to more intimate subjects. "It's been a strain on a man to be in a room, alone, with such a woman," Werner observed, taking hold of her hand and squeezing it gently between his own. "One wants to do things which…some women would feel shocked about." He paused and then asked, "How do you feel about man and woman?"

"In what way?" she asked innocently.

Werner stared blankly at her for a moment and then laughed. "That is really something. Really something!" Then he added: "Come on—how do you feel about such things?"

Krista floundered mentally for a moment before she could think of an answer. Gisela had given her enough information as to what it was necessary to say under such conditions. Finally she decided boldly to tell Werner what he expected to hear.

You have nothing to lose, her mind told her forcefully, *so why not?*

"It depends on the man and woman," Krista said. "After all, we aren't children—are we? And we didn't come up here just to hold hands."

Werner chuckled and then leaned closer, his mouth stopping only a few inches from hers. "You are delightful! Really delightful!" he told her.

For a long time neither of them moved, then he stood and took her cocktail glass. "Maybe it's time for another drink."

Krista asked, "Do you think I could handle another one of those?" She laughed to cover up her nervousness.

"I'm *sure* you can!"

He was gone, to return a few seconds later with filled glasses. As he leaned down to give Krista one, his lips brushed hers. Then he pulled away. "You're overwhelming, so very overwhelming, my child."

"Well, thank you." She smiled and took the glass, quickly taking a large swallow. The liquor flowed down her throat and settled strongly into her stomach. Moments later she felt the violent effects hammer at her head. All of a sudden everything seemed so strangely distant.

The conversation seemed to blur, and the room fell out of focus. It was the sensual feel of Werner's body against hers which stabbed awareness back. She felt a jarring sensation of his lips on hers and his tongue trying to dig past her teeth.

Suddenly, panic exploded in her mind. She was back in her stepfather's apartment, with a drunken man trying to rape her.

Without realizing what was happening, Krista jerked away from Werner, terrified. All of a sudden everything seemed horribly distorted; out of place. The world was spinning and she wanted to vomit. Krista's whole insides were bubbling violently. Then she doubled over and was sick, the choking sensation in her lungs erupting up through her throat and then out past trembling lips.

Black nausea flooded over her sight and then an ominous silence seemed to crash down, leaving nothing but a spinning dizziness to float around her awareness. She was lost in a timeless, dimensionless world which had no reality, no memory and no form. How long she was in that mystifying state, Krista didn't know. Finally it ebbed slowly away, each pulsing beat bringing more and more light, and with the light came the hammerings of pain at the side of her skull.

Suddenly Krista opened her eyes and discovered that she was lying in a strange bed, in a strange room, with Werner Pawlík beside her.

Chapter Seven

Heinz and Gisela had stayed at the nightclub for another hour after Krista and Werner had left. Then, around three in the morning, they returned to her apartment.

"Do you think Werner likes Krista?" Gisela asked as they stepped into her bedroom and closed the door after them.

"I believe so. I can't blame him. I could go for her myself."

Gisela felt a strange ache at his words, then shoved it away. There was no room for emotional feelings toward a man, and she recognized the ache. For many years she had given up the hope of finding a home and family. Her life was not constructed in such a way as to include love, merely lovers who gave money and gifts and favors. No love, because love would bring the drudgery of housework, living for a man and a man's wishes and desires. Her own independence would be crowded out, and she would become a mere slave for the man—a thing she had promised herself not to become, years before when the first man had used her for his own pleasures.

No—no love for Gisela! Yet, on the other hand, she couldn't afford to lose a good bankroll like

Heinz.

Gisela laughed and slipped out of her dress. "I don't think you would find her as interested in you as I am. She wants to get ahead. She wants out of the life of being poor and...enough of her! This isn't the time to be talking about other women...or men!" Gisela slipped out of her bra, and her breasts were freely exposed for the man's eager gaze.

Heinz let out a sigh and then stepped forward, pulling Gisela forcefully into his arms.

A thrill ebbed up through Gisela as she felt the pressure of his hard against her.

"You're right! This isn't the time for conversation," he whispered hoarsely, his lips covering hers.

She drew his tongue deep into her mouth, feeding on its sexual wine, tugging on it as if attempting to fill herself. She pressed up against the eager shape of his tongue, working hers back and forth greedily. Then it withdrew and she followed until he was voluptuously sucking on her own tongue.

When the kiss broke they were both breathing hard.

"You're a big man," she observed, wiggling a thigh against him.

"Throbbing big!" he half chuckled, letting his right hand press against the swell of one breast. "Such lovely nipples. So hard and firm. They always want to be kissed and fondled."

"I do think you have a fucking hard for me!" she observed, removing her thigh from between his legs and replacing it with the flat of her hand.

"You sure know how to treat a man great!" he announced, thrusting his hips against her caressing fingers, moving back and forth against them.

63

Both his hands were now cupping Gisela's breasts and she felt a wave of pleasure as his fingers squeezed their nipples.

"Sometimes it's fun to be just down right dirty!" she told him, grinning.

"You call this dirty?"

"Not really. Maybe sexy. Oh, you make me really hot!"

"Why don't you prove it?" he rasped huskily.

With both hands, Gisela slowly opened his pants and then anxiously exposed the naked length of his shaft. Her fingers playfully embraced his erection and lingeringly lifted and lowered up and down upon it until he was breathing even harder.

"You like that, don't you?" she asked throatily.

"What do you think?"

"I think you have a real big e prick and it just loves to have my hands caressing and moving on it."

"I like any part of you jerking my love-gun!" he assured her, eyes half lidded in the pleasure she was giving.

His hands continued to fondle and squeeze her naked breasts.

"This is thrilling!" Gisela announced. "Now isn't it?"

"As thrilling...as this?" One hand moved down between her legs and slowly lifted, touching her in such a manner that she suddenly wanted to have her clothing ripped off.

"Your pussy is hot!" he moaned in delight.

Her fingers jerked rapidly upon his shaft, erotic-ally driven by the touch of his caress.

"Oh, this is fun!" she cried.

His hand was now gathering up her skirt and finally it slipped under the cloth, quickly discovered the area where pink panties covered the fleecy heat of her groin.

"Get it naked!" she moaned. "It's really hot for you."

Now with both hands under her skirt, he pulled on her panties, fairly yanking in their desperation. Then she felt the anxious touch of his naked fingers discovering the warmth of her burning flesh.

She automatically discovered the bed, fell backward, hands drawing her skirt high about her waist. She ripped at the panties gathered about her thighs.

Then he was at her.

He had removed his own slacks and now, as he fell between her legs, she thrilled.

At that moment, Gisela lost control.

Her legs whipped about his body and she moaned. One upward thrust of her hips and he was buried deep inside her.

"Oh, Heinz, you're good, good!"

His own hips were now thrusting with hers.

"Yes, yes...oh, you're so good!" she managed to cry between clinched teeth as pleasure mounted upon pleasure with every lunging thrust of his shaft.

Orgasm shuddered through every nerve and yet he continued to penetrate her until suddenly another attack of pleasure came into being to build to a multiple climax as he reached his own limits of control.

They clung to one another for a long time, breathing hard.

How long they lay that way before moving, Gisela didn't know.

Finally they rearranged themselves on the bed, lying side-by-side, saying nothing.

Gisela was thinking about how wonderful it felt to be a woman and know the pleasure of a man doing such things to her as Heinz had just completed.

The more she thought, the greater the need to know him again became.

And suddenly she was pressing against him, rubbing up at his hips, wanting to experience the pleasure of a hard male responding to her body.

He embraced Gisela and started covering her lips with tender kisses that quickly changed to voluptuous tongue dances. They strained together tightly and she parted her thighs enough to allow move between the embrace of her legs.

"Oh, you're driving me crazy!" she sobbed against his shoulder.

All at once Gisela rolled over on top of him.

"I could keep this up all night!" she moaned tensely.

But it didn't last very long because the fires burning inside her were too great.

All at once Gisela clawed him tighter against her and then lifted up, plunged down.

As the pleasure mounted and then finally burst to almost unbearable intensity, Gisela's thoughts faded, and then returned to normal as the man moved away. They lay together for a long time.

That little Krista couldn't compete with me, Gisela thought with inner pleasure. *She could never compete!*

Then, Gisela found herself wondering why she should even be thinking such thoughts. Maybe it was because Krista was still lovely and young, innocent and pure; in mind if not in body, any longer. And with the realization came an edge of jealousy. That was followed by another emotional thought: *You won't be young and innocent much longer, Krista—not much longer will you have that edge on me! You'll become hard, and bitter toward the world—more so than you are right now. You'll become cold and calculating, until you'll have become one with me. A sister in sin, a sister in...*

The thought remained incomplete because her own basic sexual desires flared up at the touch of the man's hand on her stomach.

Giggling in delight she said: "Come on, you big stud, do your duty!"

Chapter Eight

It took Krista several seconds to realize where she was; then the shock of what had happened the night before was followed by the question of what *else* had happened.

The man sat up in bed as she moved from it.

"Are you all right?" he asked in a gentle voice.

"What?" Krista turned, startled. She didn't know quite how to act. All the careful planning and the careful conversation and outer layer of worldliness which Gisela had glossed quickly over her personality was not completely dead. She was the Krista Gustav, young girl, who didn't know the way to act in the presence of a man in his bedroom.

"You drank too much, so I put you to bed. There wasn't any place else to sleep, so...I didn't think you'd mind me being there with you."

Krista managed to recover, and quickly attempted to hide her inexperience and innocence. "I didn't realize...guess it was the drinks you gave me. I'd never had one like that before. It was terribly strong."

"I'm sorry." Werner stated, brushing a strand of thinning hair from his forehead. His eyes were traveling unconsciously along Krista's body.

Krista was startled to realize that she was wearing only her bra and panties. The exposure was far less than it might have been, yet embarrassment colored her features.

"Your clothes are in the closet. I hung them up there." Werner announced, pointing and turning his head so that he wasn't looking at her any more.

As she went and got her clothing, Werner told her how he had undressed and then put her to bed. "You were quite a sick young lady. You don't know how much of a temptation it was for me to have my way with you anyway. You're beautiful. Much more beautiful than I'd thought."

Krista's dress was wrinkled, but it served the purpose of covering her body. When she turned to look at the man again, he was staring at her. There was naked desire in his eyes. She tried to think what another woman in her situation would do. What would Gisela do? The logical thing was to let the man have her, to continue where they had started the evening before. But the thought terrified her. Something had blocked all ability to act when he had taken her in his arms. The image of Karl Roher had stabbed momentary madness through her mind and emotions. It scared Krista. What was wrong with her?

"You want me to take you home?" Werner asked, his voice bland, without any hint as to what he was really thinking or desiring; only his eyes gave vent to his thoughts and passions at the sight of her, so near.

"I *do* feel pretty bad." That was the truth, because her head was hammering madly, as if little men with steel hammers were pounding the inside of her skull in an attempt to break through it. "Guess I'm not used to so much to drink. At least the combination you gave me."

Regret was heavy in Werner's voice, even though his words were kindly and understanding. "That's all right. I know how it must be. There's nothing wrong with getting overpowered by liquor once in awhile. Everybody should have at least one or two chances to learn."

His eyes took in her figure once more as he sat up in the bed. He was thoughtful, and then finally stood and walked to the bathroom. "I'll get ready and we'll have something for breakfast. Then I'll take you back to Gisela's place."

Chapter Nine

It was several days before Werner called Krista. She had given up all hope of seeing him again. When she had told Gisela what had happened, the older girl had just nodded and said it might take time. "Some girls have to learn the hard way."

Those days were difficult ones for Krista. Each day at the office grated nervously by. It was only by having something to drink at lunchtime that she was able to continue. Then one afternoon she received a call at work from Werner Pawlík.

He quickly apologized for not having phoned sooner. "I've been quite busy. I know it's short warning, but I remembered about you being interested in modeling, and there's a small party where you might be able to meet some important people. If they are impressed, they'll be able to help you."

Her first reaction was to wonder why he should be trying to help her, after what had happened in his apartment. Yet even though he looked repulsive and unattractive, he had proved himself a gentleman in his actions toward her.

"I'd be delighted to go. What time will you pick me up?" she asked.

"About eight. We can go someplace and have a

cocktail and then talk. I'll have a few things to tell you."

"That's fine."

It was eight sharp when Werner picked her up. Gisela had helped Krista dress again, and made up her face in that haunting mixture of maturity and innocence. He commented on how beautiful she looked, then took her to a cocktail lounge which catered to American tourists and occupation troops. She had never seen such a place, and it seemed like a new world. And in her young fancy she imagined herself in America, a girl who lived in New York or Los Angeles. The place didn't matter—it was just a game, pretending she was somewhere else.

The place was dimly lighted and there were small round tables. A long bar spanned one side of the room. It was still too early for many people to be there, so they had the quiet and the darkness to give them privacy. They seated themselves in a corner booth, then Werner Pawlík ordered martinis. "You tried mine, so you can try some of these," he told her.

They sat quietly for a long time, then Werner started a casual conversation about the place. "A lot of Americans come here. Very popular. Just enough touch of the German for their tastes, and just enough American to make them feel that the surroundings are familiar and they can relax."

"You sound like you don't really think much of the Americans," Krista commented, finding it hard to bring her eyes up to his.

"It's not the Americans so much—just the ones that come here. They throw their money around as if they were trying to prove something." There was a heaviness in his voice as he spoke.

"I've come across some Americans—they were pretty nice. When I was a child I dreamed of marrying an American and going to his country to live. It was a nice dream."

"I guess you could have done a lot worse. I sell a lot of my products to the American market. It's just that I wish they could come down to earth. Take the space race. It took the Russians to make the Americans realize that they weren't the leaders in everything or could do what they damned well pleased. It served them right! The funny thing is, though, Hitler was just the same way—he didn't listen to his scientists. Maybe it's just better that way. Otherwise he might have won the war. We've never been so good since after the Second World War. So now America and Russia are competing with German scientists as their 'brains.' That's sort of ironic." Werner paused and then shook his head.

"I'm sorry. I got off in the clouds. I don't think this is so very interesting to you. After all, that's not really very romantic talk."

He smiled, and Krista felt a tenderness move through her for the man. He was quite nice, regardless of the fact that he didn't physically attract her. He couldn't help his looks, but he was in charge of his personality—as was everybody—and Werner Pawlík had done a very nice job with himself. Krista decided that she liked him after all.

The cocktails came and they sipped half the drinks before Werner turned the conversation to the subject he had mentioned on the telephone.

"Tonight we're going to a party given by Gerd Richter. He's not only a fashion designer, but a model promoter. He has his fingers in a little of everything, in fact. He'll be looking at you with only one thing in mind—whether you are good for showing off his clothing, whether you will add the finishing touch to a design which will cause buyers to want the dress. He's not interested in you as a woman. In fact, he's not interested in women, if you know what I mean."

Krista wasn't quite sure, but she nodded. She had heard about men who weren't interested in women sexually, but she didn't understand anything more about the subject.

"Just look pretty, and stick close to me. I'll see to it that you get the right attention."

"Why are you doing this for me?" Krista asked, the drink having made her a little bolder.

Werner looked into her eyes for a moment before answering. "I don't know, really. Maybe because I like you—there's a certain appeal about you—and maybe it's because I think you might have a chance as a first-rate model if handled right. Gisela said you were interested in getting into something like that, and that you were a very grateful girl." The last statement was accented slightly, and his hand reached out and folded meaningfully around hers.

A nervous flutter moved at the pit of Krista's stomach, but she smiled. There wasn't any real reason why she shouldn't reward this man for anything he might do for her. It was just the way it was done. So cold-blooded. And she couldn't kill, completely, the inner urge to make any sexual relationship beautiful, even though the act had already been made dirty and disgusting by her stepfather. A shiver shook through Krista.

"Cold?" Werner asked.

"No. Just a chill." Krista hoped that he might think it was the contact of his hand on hers. She smiled warmly at him.

They finished their drinks, then Werner looked at his wrist watch. "Well, we might as well start."

After paying the bill, he helped her out of the booth and they walked out of the lounge.

* * * * * * *

The party was held in a large hotel suite; there was a huge fake fireplace in the living room. A man stood behind a bar in the corner and mixed drinks. Another man was playing a small baby grand piano in the other corner. Already half a dozen people had arrived.

Krista was surprised at the size of the party; she had thought it would be a small group. Werner told her there were supposed to be a little over fifty people there before the evening was finished.

He led her to a tallish, thin man who had almost childlike features. There was something feminine about the way he moved and talked. His eyes jerked along Krista's figure as she stepped up to him, with Werner beside her. There was a coldness in his expression as he examined her.

"This young girl you were telling me about this afternoon, Werner?" the man asked in a high-pitched, lilting voice. His eyes hadn't left Krista; something about the way they kept sweeping up and down her body reminded her of a woman looking at another woman.

"This is the girl, Krista Gustav." Werner turned to her and said, "This is Gerd Richter."

"Good day, Mr. Richter," she greeted, smiling. She extended her hand, but he ignored it.

"Had any experience in modeling?" he coldly asked, appraising her eyes with his own. He still hadn't changed expression. The full, almost womanly lips which had asked the question had a weak look about them, belying the tone of voice and attitude which he projected.

"No," she answered honestly, "but I'm willing to work!"

Richter nodded and then finally turned his eyes toward Werner. "She's your headache, if you want to do anything with her—polish her—I'll see her then!" Abruptly his attention was turned away, and he seemed to have already forgotten them.

Werner shrugged and pulled Krista after him. They walked to the small bar. A few minutes later they were sipping brandy and standing off to one side.

"He doesn't seem very polite," Krista observed testily.

"He's a very busy man—important," Werner told her. "I think he liked you."

"What? Are you kidding me?"

"No. He said if you have a little polish, he might be interested in seeing you again. That's just as good as saying that you're in. You just have to be polished the next time. If you could get into one of his shows, you would be made in the modeling industry. I believe you could do very well. We'll see what the next weeks bring. Is that all right?" He smiled and gently squeezed her arm.

Krista couldn't help feeling he might just be playing her along, hoping to get the use of her body on promises. This was a completely new game in her life, and she didn't have any experience to draw upon in order to make realistic judgments. She would have to take Gisela's word for it all.

In the next couple of hours she was introduced to several people in the fashion business. One in particular stood out from the others. He was a tall, dark-haired man with a tanned face. He had the look of an athlete. His face was angular; his eyes had the expression of a man who has lived, and desires the fun of living—a man who took hold of life with both hands and fought for the pleasures with a violent passion. The way his dark eyes bore into Krista's as they were introduced caused an excitement to flutter through her. She didn't even hear his name or anything about him, it seemed as if she had suddenly been sliced with a knife; all her senses were cut away except for those that centered around the visual picture of the man. It was a little over an hour later that she saw him again.

Werner had gone off with someone for a few minutes when the man stepped up to Krista's side. "Well, hello. I see your friend has left you alone." He smiled warmly at Krista. He looked at her figure as though taking in a work of art. "You mind if we talk?"

"Not at all," Krista found herself saying, dazedly.

The drinks had finally blanketed over her a little, and there was a light glow of excitement which the liquor had developed. With an effort she managed to cover her eagerness to learn something

about the man, and her excitement that he had returned to talk to her.

"You know, I'm sure we met..." she managed to
say in a casual, puzzled voice.

The man smiled, then bowed his head slightly.
"Peter Schmidt. We were introduced a little while
ago." Amusement was thick in his voice.

"Oh, I'm sorry, but Mr. Pawlík has introduced
me to so many people that I guess they've been going in and out of my mind without even staying long
enough to make an impression." She hesitated, then
added: "Though I can't understand why *you* didn't
stay longer."

The man chuckled and glanced at the small bar.
"Could I get you something to drink?"

"I think that would be nice."

"Then outside, onto the balcony?" His authority
was that of a man who didn't expect a woman to
have any objections to his wishes; no room was left
for such objections. No woman *would* object! She
found herself doing as the man suggested, and they
were standing outside on the small balcony, alone,
sipping brandy and looking out over Hanover and
the dotted jewels of its night world.

"This is a beautiful town," Peter Schmidt observed, placing a gentle hand on hers. She felt a
sudden thrill at the contact, and couldn't understand
why.

"I never thought much of it."

"You must have been born here, then."

Krista nodded. "A long time ago."

Peter seemed amused. "So long as all that?"

"No. I didn't mean in years. It's just that a lot
can happen to a woman in a short time."

He was thoughtful, then nodded. "A lot has happened to our country in the last twenty years. A lot has happened to our people. A child grows up fast during wartime. I was old enough to be in the tail end of the war. It was a bitter time; many deserted.... Well, that's in the past." He turned and smiled. "You surely don't remember much about the war."

Krista smiled shyly and found herself unable to avoid an honest answer. "Very little."

"I thought so." For a little while they were silent and Krista had time to wonder what she was doing out there with a total stranger, alone, talking as if she had known him for a long time. Then he asked:

"What are you doing with a man like Werner?"

"I'm interested in getting into modeling."

"Why?"

"Get out of the trap I'm in now."

"There are other ways, much easier."

"What?"

"Get married, for one. Find a nice guy and get married. Then you don't have to lose your innocence."

"What innocence?" she demanded bitterly.

"Oh—hit a sore spot! Sorry. But you don't look like the kind of young woman who has been hurt *that* much."

"Sometimes it doesn't show in the face."

"But it's never too late to find a young man and—"

"And what would we have? Apartments aren't that easy to get. You live with his parents—if he has some. And what kind of life is that?"

"Everybody in Germany is in the same situation.

KRISTA, BY CHARLES NUETZEL

Why should you be different?"

She suddenly found herself standing more rigidly, proudly. "I'm Krista Gustav!"

"And who is Krista Gustav?" he asked pointedly.

She was stunned by his question. It was biting and humiliating. It had the edge of truth to it, and because of that it was painful. *Who was Krista Gustav?* A nobody girl from a nobody family who had been forced into a sex act by a nobody stepfather. And where was that Krista Gustav going? What was it she really wanted? Out? Out of what? A trap which her country had made for her. A trap from which there really wasn't any easy or decent escape.

"I'm a girl who wants to get ahead!" she finally managed to say in a controlled voice.

"But what will you find when you get there?" Peter Schmidt inquired gently. "Will it be all glitter and stars and gold and honey? Will there be reward and happiness at the end of your efforts—or will you merely find that it is just as empty as the beginning?" He noticed a look of apprehension cross Krista's lovely face and seemed to have regretted having been the cause of it.

"Forgive me. Perhaps it is unkind of me to say such disillusioning things, but I have had so much experience with young women such as yourself who set out to capture some magic position—one which they were sure would bring them complete happiness for all time to come. All too often these young, usually beautiful women such as yourself, found great disappointment rather than the happiness they sought. Believe me, my dear, money alone will not bring peace or happiness. You have such an innocent air, and I would hate for you to face the disappointment and emptiness others in your present position came to realize."

Krista stared carefully at the man, looking deep into his eyes and seeing something there which she hadn't noticed before.

"You sound bitter about life."

The man shrugged and took a sip of his brandy. "Like everything in the world, I've been around too long to keep my youthful outlook. That which begins hollow ends the same way. There *is* no gold at the end of the rainbow—merely some dirty colors which have been faded by eternity. It's all a circle with the individual moving along the line, always seeking something which doesn't exist because it's not in the outer world, it's inside yourself. And if you don't find it inside yourself, you'll keep looking for it outside. I never found it either place." The man paused and then smiled wryly. "Now you managed to turn the point. Very good."

"I'm sorry," Krista managed to say. "It *has* gotten a little stiff for strangers, hasn't it?"

Peter nodded, then gripped her hand. "I hope you'll let that come to an end. I'd like to know you better."

Krista felt excitement flow over her. His eyes were dark and haunting, probing deep into hers. He was once again that dynamic personality which had stepped up to her a few minutes before. Overwhelming in his male appeal and power over her.

"I'd like that, too."

"May I see you again?"

Krista nodded, unable to hide her interest and excitement any longer.

"Good! Wonderful!" he exclaimed.

When he asked for her address, she eagerly gave it to him. Then they returned to the apartment and he suddenly disappeared. Half an hour later, Werner returned.

"Having fun?"

Krista shrugged. "I could do better."

"We'll go, pretty soon. It's getting late."

It was a little over half an hour before they finally left the party. Krista didn't see Peter Schmidt again during that time, but his image and effect were still working on her mind and body as they drove toward Werner Pawlík's home.

As they entered his rooms, no excuse was made or explanation offered. It had already been assumed this would be their final destination, and no comment was needed. He closed the door and offered Krista a drink.

She accepted the brandy he gave her and downed it in the next few minutes, asking for another. It seemed as if she were going through a dream world that had only a dim reality to it. All her thoughts were centered on Peter Schmidt. She had never met a man like him before, and she doubted that very many women ever did. There was a certain demanding quality about him which fascinated and overwhelmed a woman. She could not think about Werner as even an important or terrifying factor, at the moment. Right now what was going to happen would be something that had to be done—but done in a detached, faraway manner.

The brandy burned away most of Krista's mental reluctance and she sat there, quietly waiting, not even hearing what the man was telling her.

When they got up to go into his bedroom, she wasn't quite sure if this were the right thing to do. But there was no real escape. It was like living in a kind of fantastic dream. Somehow it was an exciting dream, yet in another way it was frightening.

The way the man had looked at her during the conversation was boldly sexual, as if he were stripping her body naked and mentally caressing and kissing her flesh.

That though had been erotic.

Yet she was frightened deep down inside.

Because this was going to be her first experience with a man under conditions which she actually accepted and she wasn't even really caring much, or aware of how it was happening. There was a sense of reluctant acceptance, a sense of realizing it was necessary to learn how to deal with just this kind of situation, without letting it pervert or hurt her inner core. This was going to be a necessary part of her future, if she wanted to get out of the deep hole which life had dug for her. This was her way out; the only one she could imagine. She had to learn how to make the most of it.

Krista found herself moving as if in a daze, being led like a small child.

She felt suddenly helpless and little. Tiny. Without strength or will.

When he pulled her into his arms, standing in front of the bed, she was sharply aware of the excitement thrusting through him. The feel of his hips, the hardness pressing so bluntly there both excited and frightened Krista.

She remembered what had happened with her stepfather and an inner shudder raced down her spine. Was it going to be like that? Or could it be possible that she'd actually discover pleasure in this man's arms?

The questions and thoughts blurred as her lips met his in an open-mouthed kiss.

As his tongue probed deeply within the confines of her mouth, Krista felt a strange wave of pleasure.

Yet this was not a new sensation. She had been kissed in this manner before and responded.

Still the tenseness of his mannish form against hers, the awareness of his shaft hard and stiff touching her stomach created a sense of hesitation.

"Oh, Krista, you are beautiful to kiss," he told her tenderly as their lips parted. Then he gently caressed her cheek with his mouth, found her ear, toyed with the lobe with the point of his tongue.

Another pleasure-wave made her weak.

He was so strong, so dominating and tender at the same time. Could it be for real the feelings touching her body?

She remembered some of the things her roommate had said about men. How they liked to have their erections caressed by a woman's hands, kissed by her lips.

The thought stunned Krista, since it seemed certain that such acts would be impossible for her to offer a man.

Then Werner lifted her up in his arms and gently lay her on the bed, his hands playing along her body in lingering gentle touches, just lightly glancing over her breasts which thrust up against the bra. The nipples immediately responded, hurting against the cloth.

A sigh lifted her breasts and lowered them as he

once again caressed across their points.

"Sure a lovely woman," he said in a dreamy voice.

Werner's eyes gazed down into hers with a burning fire of tenderness, mixed with raw desires, as if the passions which he had been controlling all evening were finally being given a more blunt freedom of expression.

"I've never known a woman quite like you before, Krista! You are beautiful beyond all women that I've known. There's something about you which casts a spell of desperation and desire over a man. I... I..." His lips were coming toward hers and she felt the gentle touch of his hand as it cupped over one covered breast.

The boldness of his touch was surprisingly pleasant. It felt so good that Krista didn't want him to ever stop touching her in that way.

The realization startled her.

This was so different from what she'd expected. Both passionate and romantic. And those words had held an odd conviction that made it impossible to keep from believing him.

Yet why should he feel this way about her? What made her special?

Then their lips met and his were gentle as they covered hers.

She thrilled to that contact.

This was so gentle. So loving. The emotion that filled Krista seemed to cloud all thoughts of what would follow. This was a simple kiss.

Then his mouth opened and she willingly responded, drawing his tongue deeply past her teeth, thrilling.

She kept thinking how delightfully strange and wonderful the kiss felt. But it was difficult to know for sure if it was the drinks or the physical desire of her body; or possibly a response to his words.

Then as his hand fondled, squeezed her breast, Krista felt a wild tremor rush through her. And now she knew it was a physical response, erotic.

Up to that point she had been, for the most part, responsive, submissive, only.

Now her own hands touched and caressed his shoulders, neck, and her body pressed up alongside his, thrilled by the nearness, the thrust of his tongue filling her mouth.

Every nerve seemed to be slowly burning, firing like she had never experienced.

With dates in the past there had never been such a thrilling pleasure at a mere kiss. Krista realized that her excitement was partly swelling beyond control because this time it would be all the way—no stops.

In the first moments she was merely aware of her breasts being caressed and her mouth being moistly explored. And the feel and touch of the man.

And slowly a desire to be totally naked, to feel his touch on her bare flesh was almost overwhelming. Her lungs were already gasping for breath and her mouth trembling with excitement. It was then she realized that the mental image of Peter Schmidt was before her mind, exciting her. For a moment panic raced over her nerves, then she focused the younger man's image over that of Werner. No feeling of guilt or strangeness entered her mind.

In the next moments Krista was merely aware of

the man's hands running over the length of her body, across her stomach, down into the heat of her groin that was suddenly highly responsive to a sensual caress.

She trembled under the touch and felt herself automatically press up against the fingers.

When his hand clutched her groin in a more meaningful way, letting one finger slip along the lines of her love-lips, a soft murmur of pleasure uttered from her throat as the welling sensual need thrilled every nerve.

Suddenly she realized that somehow Werner had managed to remove her clothing, but couldn't remember his doing so. It was as if that portion of time had been cut away or that her sensual awareness of being touched had blended out all knowledge of having been undressed.

The acceptance of this startled her for only a moment. Then she forgot as the man began covering her breasts with kisses.

The nipples were stiff and erected and his tongue played them back and forth.

A sob passed her teeth and trembling lips. "Oh, God, it's good!

At that point she became aware of the tip of his erected penis touching her thigh and a sharp intake of breath lifted her breasts against his lips.

Then she felt his lips searching for hers and a stab of wonderful pleasure exploded through her as he pressed down against her.

Krista's mind spun in a sea of sensation.

It was happening and seemed totally different from what she expected.

Her own hips automatically reached up, lifted,

moved against the maleness of his hard, which worked slowly up and down in a lingeringly lovely rhythm that excited her beyond control.

All at once Krista couldn't wait.

A murmur broke from her lips. Her body was now writhing under his in its eager need. Every nerve was burning raw, and she wanted to continue feeling the hardness of his shaft moving against her.

Never had she experienced such excitement and release from emotional restraints.

And suddenly the man's crown was searching entrance into her body. She lifted, helped awkwardly and gasped when the thickness of him found her, surging slowly in until the full length of that hard shaft was tightly buried within her.

"Oh, oh, that...feels...wonderful!" she gasped in ecstatic pleasure.

Each thrust, each penetration sent shivers of pleasure through her body.

It was so different from the ugly experience with her stepfather.

This was what it should be all about, her mind cried in joy.

Her own hips moved in response to the man's and she found herself clutching to his shoulders, pressing her chest up so that his would touch her nipples.

The man had no name, no shape other than the feel of him inside her; and the touch of his shoulders an chest against her nipples.

It was a nameless male, sensually taking her through an erotic experience of such pleasure that it didn't matter who the person behind the body was.

All sensation was trapped to the sensual experience. Nothing more mattered.

Then all at once the man strained downward and the world exploded in pleasure, as if some heavenly thing had plugged her into a socket of ecstasy, bathing all the golden music and all the golden beauty of the world over her body and through her soul. A mounting beauty of love raced through her with caressing care; with wild, wonderfully fulfilling perfection. Her mind screamed out a name over and over again, in rhythm with the man's thrusts. *Peter, Peter, Peter, Peter....*

Then the bath of joy washed away and she was lying in the aftermath, exhausted and happy, knowing she had discovered for the first time in her life a perfection of love, a knowledge of what relations between man and woman could be like, should be like.

It didn't occur to her that it was Werner Pawlík who had given this to her; it didn't enter her mind that it was his hands, his kisses, his body which had moved her upward through a mounting world of sensual joy and perfection. She only saw the image of Peter Schmidt, and believed it was this which had made it possible for her to go through the degrading experiment, the degrading act which otherwise would have been impossible to endure.

It was a long, long time before sleep settled over Krista, and with it came dreams of Peter Schmidt. She lived through a whole romance with this "dream lover" of hers, and when morning came she awakened gladly to the world of reality, still in a joyful mood of happiness and contentment.

Chapter Ten

Krista and Gisela were sitting at the breakfast table talking, a couple of days later. It was the first chance that Krista had to talk in detail about what had happened to her during the evening with Werner. She had just told the other woman about having met a Mr. Peter Schmidt.

Gisela's eyes went large and her expression showed open amazement. "You don't mean *the* Peter Schmidt?"

"You mean there is such a...*the* Peter Schmidt?" Krista asked, startled by the other woman's reaction.

Gisela laughed nervously and then said: "There's a tall, dark, good-looking guy who has more money than he knows what to do with. He manufactures clothing for world distribution. He is also famous for his affairs with women." Gisela brushed back a lock of dark hair and took another strong sip of her black coffee. "If this is the same man, you really hit a big find! If he wasn't just giving you a line."

"What if...if this is who he is?" Krista wanted to know, suddenly filled with a confusion of fear. She would never know how to act with such a man

Before, it had been different. But it would be

impossible now, knowing who he was.

"You just play along. If you play right you'll really be in a good position. He has more contacts than anybody else. If he gets interested, you tag onto the guy! You won't need Werner Pawlík any more. You won't need anybody except Peter Schmidt He has made several famous models out of nobodies. If he gets romantically involved with a woman, there's no telling how far he might take her." Gisela's voice was filled with awe and excitement, and the emotion reached Krista.

"You'll have to get yourself fixed up even more. That hair; like I said before, you should have it bleached. Then you'll have that finishing touch you need. Tonight I'll take care of it."

That evening Gisela made good her promise, and even though Krista was hesitant about letting the other woman do anything so drastic as changing the color of her hair, she realized it was for the best.

She was amazed when she looked into the mirror. She couldn't believe that she was seeing the same Krista Gustav. The lighter hair color seemed to change her whole appearance. Where before she had been made up to look worldly, with a mixture of innocence, she now had the look of a woman of about twenty-five who knew her way around any situation.

"You don't think it looks cheap?" Krista asked.

"No. It looks...well, soft and caress able. If I were a man I believe I'd find you even more irresistible."

Krista turned happily to Gisela. "You don't know how much you have meant to me! You've done so much, and asked nothing in return. Why?"

"Because I'm a human being. Maybe because I think about the girl I used to be. I don't know. It's hard for a girl to get along nowadays; easier than a few years ago, but still hard enough. You need help from somebody."

"But what do you get out of it?" Krista turned and looked at herself in the mirror again. Her fingers played with her hair, touching it as if for the first time.

"Satisfaction, I guess," Gisela stated. Then she laughed. "Let's not talk about *that!* Let's just hope Mr. Schmidt calls."

Not too many thoughts centered around Werner Pawlík, and Krista was almost startled to receive a call from him the next day at work.

"There's a man who wants to see you this evening—he's going to help you on a few pointers. I'll pick you up around seven. We'll go to my place then."

* * * * * * *

"You look lovely tonight," Werner told Krista as they stepped into his apartment. "And I like that change of hair color. I'd hardly recognize you."

He led her to the sofa and mixed drinks for them. His favorite martinis. As he sat down next to her, he said, "I guess you're wondering the reason for the sudden call."

Krista nodded, taking the glass he offered her and sipping from it. "It *was* a little sudden."

Werner placed a gentle hand on her leg and sighed happily and a little tiredly. "The business world is a little wild. You don't know how wonderful it is to be here with you. We'll have to get together more often." He relaxed for a moment, then said: "This man called me last night and asked to see you. He's in a very good position to help you. Has a lot of money, and it's a hobby of his, I'm told, to help young women. Just don't let yourself get too involved!" Werner patted Krista's leg once more, this time quite intimately. "You're my girl, don't forget!"

"When is he coming?" she asked. She had come to the conclusion that she liked Werner, but nothing more. The man had turned out to be much nicer than he had seemed at first. But that was as far as it went.

"Who is it that's coming?"

"You met him the other night. Peter Schmidt."

The rest of the conversation was lost to Krista in her excitement. How long it was before the doorbell rang, she didn't know, for she was spinning in a daze of anticipation, which had to be hidden from Werner.

"Hello," he answered. "I was hoping that you would remember me. Our meeting was so brief the other evening, I thought you might not remember." The tone of his voice indicated that he wished to keep secret their private meeting.

A drink was mixed and handed to Peter. He sipped it carefully, his dark eyes keeping contact with Krista's. He spoke to Werner "She's more lovely than I remembered. She looks different!" His voice held approval.

"She lightened her hair. It does things for her, I think," Werner said with obvious pride. It was almost fatherly pride.

Krista wondered why it was that he wanted to

help her. Again the question of his motives entered her mind, bringing doubt.

"You say she never had any training, but with her looks and figure I don't believe she needs much. Stand up, Krista, and walk across the room." Peter made a motion with his hand. "Walk slowly, as if you were showing off that dress you are wearing."

Krista stood and carefully walked across the room, moving as if she were walking on eggs and afraid of breaking them.

"No—not so stiffly. Relax a little. Hold your head a little higher. Don't look at the floor," Peter instructed her. "Look directly in front of you— that's right."

For the next fifteen minutes Peter Schmidt put her through a series of practices, walking from one end of the room to another, then finally he nodded. "You'll shape up into a fine model with very little training. You follow instructions very well."

Krista smiled her thanks, then sat down and finished her martini. The conversation turned to other subjects for a time, then finally returned to Krista. "I understand," Peter announced, "that you want to get out of the work you're in. I could hire you. You could come to work at my office for a couple of weeks; there you'd have more of a chance to get more personal attention."

She felt a little uneasy. It seemed strange that they should be taking such interest in her. She was a nobody, and they were taking their time to help. It couldn't *all* be Gisela's influence.

Arrangements were made for her to come to Schmidt's office to work the next Monday. Peter said he knew the Company Manager of the place she worked, and would arrange things so she could get away without any notice. When it was around eleven he offered to take her home.

Werner cut in quickly. "That's all right. I can take care of her, Peter."

Krista saw a flicker of disappointment in Peter's eyes, which mirrored her own inner feelings. She managed to hide her regret, and forced a tight smile. "I'll see you at the office Monday," she said. "And thanks." She extended her hand, waiting with an inner tension for the contact of his hand. They touched for only a moment, then Peter was gone.

Once the door was closed behind the man, Werner turned to Krista. "I think he likes you. I only hope you don't forget me."

Krista smiled. "How could I forget you?"

Werner stepped forward without another word; his lips covered Krista's. The kiss was startlingly pleasant. She responded fully, pressing her body up against his. After a moment he moved away, taking her hand and going into the bedroom.

There was something wonderful about the whole thing that Krista found almost difficult to accept. It seemed like a fantasy.

Never once did Werner let her feel as if this were something cheap; yet it was.

Right from the beginning as he lay down next to her, letting his hands glide across the shape of her body, touching, caressing, discovering all the beautiful places to caress, she was only able to respond in a manner almost alien to her past experiences.

He traced his fingers along the length of her thighs, lingering just long enough to let her know the intent of his desires, yet never once giving the impression that anything other than great concern over her feeling were of prime importance.

"Oh, good!" she whispered as his fingers lingered between her thighs. Impulsively her body arched up and he gently caressed her.

Then his lips discovered one breast, lightly kissing, gently tonguing the nipple as if it were the most beautiful thing in the world.

She sighed, felt weak all over.

And he was kissing her shoulder, a hand gathered about one breast, another discovering the warmth of her groin in such a gentle thrilling movement that Krista was dazed by the pleasure that soothed through every nerve.

She suddenly reached around his shoulder, touching, aware of the firmness of his muscles.

"Oh, you are wonderful!" she told him, drawing his lips down to hers.

Impulsively she slipped her tongue between his lips and felt a wave of excitement.

She urged him onto her and he slowly answered her call, allowing his hips to gently touch hers.

They continued to kiss and when she drew his tongue greedily between her lips, a voluptuous stab of passion jerked through every muscle.

From then on it was so beautiful because Werner never once hurried, letting the motions of their bodies rock slowly together so she was aware of every delicious sensation of his deep love-caressing within her.

Later, overwhelmed with joy at what he had given, Krista found herself leaning over his hips, tenderly kissing him in a most erotic way.

She felt lustful. She wanted to give him pleasure, in a way of thanking the man for having helped her so much.

He urged her hips above him and orally made love to the burning fires building there.

It was the first time in her life that Krista really understood the full meaning of such love-making. Before it had been a kind of sexual act performed through a mist of liquor or necessity to prove to the man she was good. Now it became an act of love-making, motivated by the longing desire to give pleasure as a gift of love.

This time it was almost frantic as they met in voluptuous passion, unable to control the need that their oral love-making had created.

And during the next hour, he made passionate and careful love to Krista; and she was surprised to discover how wonderful it could be. Lustfully great!

The one time before had been clouded with the image of Peter Schmidt, a vision so vivid that she hadn't been actually aware of Werner's technique. The same should have been true this time, yet Werner's forceful lovemaking covered over her body and mind so completely, smothering all other thoughts and images, leaving Krista confused and unsure of herself.

She found herself writhing wildly under his caresses and kisses until ecstasy blurred all reality.

It was a long time before awareness filtered through her tired mind; and with it came a strange confusion of questioning about herself.

What inner physical need had possessed her body? How could she so easily have learned to find such pleasure in the physical act of man and woman, after having been so brutally raped by her step-father?

Finally rest came to her nerves. The next morning, Werner drove her to Gisela's, where she quickly changed. Then he took her to work.

That afternoon Krista was called into the Company Manager's office and told that she was free to leave that Friday.

The next days were easy for Krista—much easier than she would have thought possible.

On Friday, Werner took her out; they ended in his apartment for the night and most of that weekend. She found it a disquieting relationship between Werner and herself, and was glad when he brought her back on Saturday afternoon.

The rest of the weekend drifted quickly by, and when Monday morning finally came, she started for the offices of *Schmidt, Ltd.,* not knowing for sure what the future might bring, but finding an overwhelming excitement at the prospect of what it might hold. It was the first time since Krista had left her stepfather's home that she was honestly happy and anxious about the future.

She was now an experienced woman, and somewhat more polished than she had been so short a time before. Now things were different. And she looked at the future with great excitement.

Chapter Eleven

When Krista walked into the building which held Schmidt, Ltd., she didn't have any idea what kind of business or what kind of employment she was entering. All she realized was that a man, who must have come from a storybook about princes and princesses, had given her an escape from a world filled with memories she wished to forget. What the salary might be wasn't of importance. This was a new adventure, a new experience; something which was sure to change her life and make things somehow wonderful and complete; something which would finally give her the beginnings of paradise. It wasn't important *how* the magician performed his miracles—only that he did! It didn't matter what the price, as long as you were somehow transformed into a princess in paradise, given the castle and all the riches of the kingdom. Cinderella didn't question the fairy Godmother as to how she changed a pumpkin into a coach—she accepted. Yet Krista couldn't help wondering why. But she pushed that question aside, to be asked and answered later, when the time came.

The building was made up of many offices and many floors, holding a multitude of businesses. She was surprised to discover that *Schmidt, Ltd.* occupied the entire fifth floor of the building. Leaving the elevator, Krista found herself facing a huge glass door, with the name *Schmidt, Ltd. World Enterprises. Import and Export.* For a moment she hesitated, then took a deep breath and opened the door, stepping carefully inside.

She was facing a long counter beyond which were scores of desks and at least fifty men and women busily working. Nobody noticed her.

A feeling of depression settled over Krista. She had expected to find Peter Schmidt waiting for her, and that he would give her a private office next to his. That was part of the dream. The fantasy of a young, unsophisticated girl. Reality was something so different.

Finally she stepped to the counter and attracted the attention of a tall, elderly woman.

"I'm Miss Gustav. Herr Schmidt told me to come here today for work."

The woman stared at Krista. "I don't know anything about it." She turned and went off.

Krista got the attention of several other people and explained to them, but nobody seemed to know anything. Finally she sat down on a chair and waited. Somebody *had* to know something about her. For a long time she sat there completely ignored, then it occurred to Krista that perhaps she was expected to report to Peter Schmidt personally.

Standing, she moved to the counter. "Where would I find Mr. Schmidt's office?" she inquired of the first person whose attention she happened to get.

The man looked at her for a moment. "Back that way. But do you have an appointment?" He pointed

100

beyond him, past all the desks.

"I believe so," Krista replied timidly.

She seemed to be lost in a fantastic complex, with no road map. She followed the man's instructions on how to get to Schmidt's office, moving past desks and people, feeling a nervousness hammering in her heart. She seemed to be on inspection. All the romantic image had been shattered, and Krista felt like a little girl lost and helpless in a strange and alien world; everything was new and different and unfriendly.

Making her way to a series of enclosed offices, it was several minutes before she found the one marked *Peter Schmidt.* A moment passed before she had the courage to move forward. The large room behind her, buzzing with activity, seemed to make the man who owned this business gigantic in size. Unapproachable. He wasn't the handsome, glamorous lover of her daydreams any more; he was a huge giant who held the lives and destinies of scores— maybe hundreds of thousands—of people in his hands. What had made her think such a man had time for a nobody girl like herself?

Then she remembered their first meeting and his obviously intimate interest in her. Krista's mind focused on how he had been then and at the other meeting, in Werner's apartment. He hadn't been a man to be in awe of, or afraid of. Why should he be any different here, in his business world?

Boldly, Krista opened the door and stepped into the office.

The room was neat and modern. A large desk sat to one side of a door marked "private," and a mature woman, attractively dressed and with a very businesslike manner and appearance, looked up from her typewriter.

"Yes?" Her tone was friendly, but careful.

"I'm Krista Gustav. Mr. Schmidt is expecting me."

The woman looked puzzled, then said: "I have no record of an appointment with anybody of that name."

Suddenly Krista felt like crying, screaming, running and never coming back. She felt all the terror and loneliness of a small child who has been lost from its parents. Where to turn next?

"Well, could you tell him I'm here?" Krista inquired in a shaking voice.

The woman stared at her for a long time, then smiled. "He's not in right now."

"When do you expect him?"

"I don't know. He hasn't called in yet. He usually calls before arriving. But on Mondays one never knows when he might come in. A long weekend, usually." The woman's voice was now strangely kind sounding, as if she had guessed something of the way Krista felt about Peter Schmidt and was trying to warn her. Maybe she *did* guess about Krista and Peter, and was used to such events between her employer and girls. "If you want, you can wait here for him."

Krista noticed a small leather couch, and settled into it gratefully.

For a long time she waited, wondering when the man would arrive and what he would say when he saw her. What kind of reception would she get? It all seemed strange and oddly foreboding that he hadn't even told his secretary about her. Was she that unimportant to him?

It was a little over an hour before the office door opened and Peter Schmidt walked in. At first he didn't notice her. He said to his secretary, "I want that American contract in my office as soon as possible, Elka."

The woman nodded and turned her head toward Krista. "This woman has been waiting for you. Says you're expecting her."

Peter turned and stared blankly at Krista. Slowly his eyes came into focus.

"Oh, my God! I forgot all about you!" He quickly motioned Krista into his private office, following her. When the door closed behind them he walked to the large, clean-topped, oak desk which was placed in the middle of the small, neat office.

"Sit down. I'll be with you in a moment."

Krista watched him working in the next few minutes, and the awe and romantic picture swelled into full scope in her mind once again. He flicked switches on the communications box on the desk, talking to different employees about business deals, not stopping from one conversation to another, just flicking another switch and continuing.

Finally he relaxed and leaned back in his swivel chair, gazing tiredly at the ceiling. His large strong hands covered his face for a moment. Finally a tired sigh broke from his lips, and for the first time Krista realized that he must have been terribly busy over the weekend. But with what? Business, or a woman? It was impossible to tell. At last he turned his eyes toward Krista.

"I'm terribly sorry about this. Should have arranged things on Friday for you. Once I'd called your chief, I forgot all about it. No excuse. Just business problems; heavy ones. Hasn't been time for anything else." He leaned forward, placing his elbows on the desk top and clasping his hands together. Those dark eyes bore impersonally into hers. It was the tough businessman who thoughtfully stared at Krista. For a time he didn't say anything. Then he broke the silence. "Tell me, what can you do?"

Krista was startled by the question, and for a moment couldn't think of an answer. She just stared back into his tired, reddened eyes, wondering. Then, realizing he was waiting for an answer, she said: "I'm only trained for the poorest of office work." A thought came to her mind. She wanted something better, a good chance to get ahead, just in case nothing happened with the modeling. She had to look logically and realistically toward the future. This was a new life she was entering into, and it was possible to get lost in such a vast business. If he happened to forget about her desires in modeling, as he had forgotten about her coming to the office this morning, then it would be better to make sure she got a position that would be worth her efforts—one with a possible future. There was no telling how long Werner Pawlík might remain romantically interested in her; when that ended, everything would crumble.

"I'm able to learn fast, and *really* I don't want to be trapped in an office job. I mean, just a mere office job. I want to have something to look forward to."

Peter frowned, puzzled. "Thought you were interested in modeling. It shouldn't make any difference what you do here. I merely brought you here so that you would be free for instruction and helped in modeling. What you do here will just be to help out, when you aren't busy doing something else." He sighed, and then said: "Are you hungry?"

"What?" The question was so out of place that she couldn't understand the connection. It took several seconds for Krista to realize that there *wasn't* any connection. "I had a small breakfast. But that was several hours ago."

"Well, how about some lunch?"

"I'd love it!" Excitement overcame her hesitancy.

"You can type?"

"Yes."

His sudden changes of subject were a little unsettling, but she had already begun to get used to it.

"Would you like to work with Miss Goke?"

"Who?"

"My secretary, Elka."

"That would be wonderful!"

"That would put you close by. Elka could use a personal assistant." Peter Schmidt stood, indicating the interview was over. "We go to lunch in an hour if you can wait that long. I have something to take care of first. Go out and tell Elka you're to work with her. Have her bring in a typing desk. Then she can come in here. I have some letters to dictate."

Krista stood and walked to the door.

"Hold your head higher!" Peter scolded her.

"Thanks," she murmured, turning and smiling.

The man smiled back, this time as a man—the man she had first met.

Turning happily, Krista walked through the now

opened door to Miss Goke.

* * * * * * *

When Peter Schmidt took her to the *Luisen-Hof,* she was a little startled. The place actually scared her. It was one of the most expensive restaurants in Hanover, with heavy wooden tables covered with white linen, waiters in dark suits, a quiet, sedate atmosphere, and beautiful flower arrangements. It overwhelmed her for a few minutes. Then Peter managed to make her feel at ease, and she began to relax.

He ordered two glasses of expensive Weinbrand. "This will take care of any nervousness," he laughed lightly. "And add to your hunger."

There was a long, heavy silence until the waiter brought the Weinbrand. As they sipped from the glasses, Peter looked across at her and smiled warmly. "You *are* really a lovely young lady." Then he dropped his eyes to the glass in his hands. "I'm truly sorry about the mess things were in when you got to the office. Did you enjoy your work?"

Krista laughed nervously. "Do people really *enjoy* work?"

He smiled wryly. "I guess not. Anyway, you won't be on *that* job for long. I just had to give you something, quick, to get you off my back for awhile. In the next few days I'll arrange for you to get started learning something about modeling and put you in the next show. It's scheduled two weeks from now. Think you can learn what's necessary in that time?"

"Do you think so?" she inquired, countering his

106

question.

Peter smiled in amusement, merely turning up the corners of his lips. "You'll do. It'll give you experience. After a month you'll be on your own. I believe you'll make a lot of money when you get started."

"Why?" Krista asked, testing. "Why are you doing all this for me?"

"Oh, just say you're an attractive young woman—and then, there's always money to be made from such promotions. I'll sign you to a contract. Werner will want a cut, too, so don't think we're doing it just for fun!"

She was startled by his statement, but relieved too. "I'm *that* attractive?"

He laughed lightly and patted her hand. "Also, like I said when we first met, I want to know you better—if it's all right with you."

"Why wouldn't it be?"

"Werner Pawlík!"

"What's he got to do with it?"

"Doesn't he have the inside track?"

"I don't see how!"

"He saw you first. And I believe he's more than just mildly interested in you." His voice was probing, as if attempting to see just how involved she was with Werner.

"He doesn't have his name on me!"

"I think he would like to."

Krista didn't know what to say, so she remained quiet. It was a long time before the conversation picked up, and this time it was general. The food came; they ate in silence. Afterward Peter ordered brandy for them, and a little later they returned to his office.

Krista was busy typing for the rest of the day. When she returned home, there was a call from Werner Pawlík.

"How'd you like your new job?" he asked over the phone.

"I don't know yet."

"Tired?"

She considered that for a moment. It would be much nicer to be with Peter Schmidt this evening— but that wasn't even a possibility. She was tired, but didn't have thy heart to turn the man down.

"No!"

"Want to come over?"

She accepted, and Werner picked her up an hour later and took her to his apartment.

The evening was spent in light conversation, and ended as usual, without any awkward buildups, in the bedroom. When the time came, they just went in and undressed.

But there was no pleasure for Krista this time. Her nerves were too edgy to respond fully to the man's caresses. It was with effort that she hid her lack of interest. It seemed as if she were degrading herself and Werner, in that all her thoughts were centered around Peter Schmidt.

Each time she felt his shaft against her flesh it was that of a nameless lover without any personality.

The change in herself and her attitudes about sex was surprising.

Even as she was smothering herself between his thighs, it was a mere automatic action without emotional feelings.

Yet in a way it was always this with Werner.

What made it even more frustrating was the fact that she didn't care. This brought into focus the acceptance that she'd become something totally different from what had been the Krista of a few months before.

But for the most part there was room for only one man in her heart and mind and emotions. It was then that Krista decided she would do anything and everything in her power to win Peter.

Chapter Twelve

She was called into Peter's office. It had been three days since any personal contact had been made between the two of them outside of business, and in her inner disbelief that this could all be happening to her, Krista had begun to doubt that it would develop any further.

"Well, have we been keeping you busy?" he asked, looking up from his desk.

"Enough," Krista offered, smiling as invitingly as possible. Every day Krista had been wearing tight-fitting blouses in an attempt to catch his eye. The one she was wearing today was low cut, open at the top so that the jutting of her breasts was as revealing as she dared allow it to be.

He noticed, much to her pleasure. His eyes moved to the valley between her breasts and a smile curled on his lips. "I don't know how I've been able to ignore you so long," he muttered, half to himself. "There must be something wrong with me!" Then Peter laughed. "Anyway, that won't be for long!" He motioned her into a chair. Then his hand flipped a switch on his communication box on the desk before him. "Miss Heinisch, would you please come to my office?"

A low voice answered, and he turned his attention to Krista. "Well, this is the day I get to start you on your way. Might seem strange the way things have been moving so slowly, but we have tight schedules, and it's never easy to fit something new into them." He paused as his eyes took in the thrust of her breasts once more. "You seem to be more and more attractive every time I see you."

"Thanks. It seems all you do is tell me how you think I look. Don't you think that a girl would like something more?"

His eyebrows raised slightly. "My, you are getting to be the bold young lady now. Next thing you'll be asking me out for dinner."

"Maybe that's not such a bad idea, at that," she countered throatily.

He was about to say something when the office door opened and a tall, mannishly dressed woman in her late thirties stepped into the room.

Peter stood. "Miss Heinisch, this is Krista Gustav, the young woman I was telling you about. Sure you'll know what to do with her. I want her coached and put in the show coming up."

Miss Heinisch turned her gray blue eyes toward Krista; they ran up and down her figure approvingly. "She has the looks. I'll work things out."

"Will you go with her?" Peter suggested. "I'll see you later. We'll have to go out on the town one of these days soon." His face and voice were thick with intimate promise.

In moments Krista was following Miss Heinisch down the hallway to her office. The woman watched her silently for a long time. When they were in the privacy of a large office, one wall of which was a floor-to-ceiling mirror, she turned to Krista with a strange look in her eyes.

"You are a very attractive woman. Have you ever been in this business before?" There was a lowness to the woman's voice which startled Krista.

"No!"

The woman frowned, brushing a lock of brownish hair from her narrow forehead. She was thoughtful for a moment, and then said, "Walk across the room for me—let me see how you carry yourself."

Krista walked.

"No—no! That's not the way. How do you expect people to...Hold your head up! Wait!" Miss Heinish walked over to her desk and picked up a book. "Well, we have to start from the beginning, using the old standby. A book on the head!"

She stepped to Krista's side and took hold of her arm. Her fingers accidentally dug into Krista's breast. The woman tensed. "*Meine Lieve*—you *are* very lovely!" Then she placed the book on Krista's head. "Try walking across the room now."

For the next hour she was forced to walk back and forth until she was able to balance the book for as long as demanded. All the time the woman's eyes seemed to take in her body, rather than what she was doing. Strange feelings and thoughts raced through Krista's mind every time her eyes made contact with Miss Heinisch's. It seemed almost as if a man were looking at her. The eyes had an odd inner expression in them which was unsettling.

Finally, when the woman was satisfied that Krista had done enough of that exercise, she stepped up to her. For a moment they stared at one another, then Miss Heinisch stepped back.

"Would you like a brandy?"

It was a strange request, and Krista didn't know exactly how to handle it.

"For your nerves. I've put you through quite a spell," the older woman offered, having noticed her puzzlement.

"Thanks. I could use one."

As the woman went to her desk and opened the drawer, Krista took a pack of cigarettes from her purse and a few moments later was dragging deeply; it tasted good to her.

Miss Heinisch went to the door and locked it. "Don't want to be disturbed. It wouldn't go well for anybody to know we were drinking on duty," she explained, smiling.

There was a low couch in the corner of the room, and she indicated they could sit there, while she got some cups from the water cooler. Krista sat down tiredly, half closing her eyes. The workout of the last hour was more of a strain on her nerves than she had realized. When the woman sat down next to her, she didn't actually notice how close it was, or that a thigh pressed against hers.

"Here—drink up."

Krista took the cup of brandy and gulped on it. For a moment after the woman refilled the now empty cup, she wondered vaguely about herself. In the past weeks her drinking habits had been far more pronounced than in the past. Then the thought faded away as the liquor soothed over her nerves.

Miss Heinisch's hand dropped to Krista's thigh in a seemingly innocent gesture of friendliness. "I didn't mean to work you so hard, dear," the woman

113

said.

"That's all right, Miss Heinisch. I expect that," Krista quickly assured her, taking another sip of the brandy.

"Call me Ingrid. We don't have to be formal. In fact. I'd much rather we were very close friends. Very, very close!" Her voice was quite low, and her lips were near Krista's ear. "I've known a lot of girls, and never have I seen one prettier than you. Such a body! Your breasts are firm and youthful. So lovely."

Krista was a little surprised at the drift of the conversation, but didn't actually think it was out of the ordinary, as a more experienced woman might.

Ingrid Heinisch suddenly moved away and then said, as if it had just occurred to her, "My gosh! I just realized. I didn't get a fitting of you."

"A what?" Krista demanded, alarmed.

"I have to have your measurements! So they can fit designs to you." Ingrid stood and reached for Krista. "Could you take off your blouse, your skirt?"

"Why?"

"So I can measure you."

Krista accepted it, not noticing the huskiness and eagerness of the woman's voice and actions. Ingrid's eyes were already stripping her bare.

In moments Krista had stripped down to bra and panties. Ingrid's eyes lighted with an inner glow at the sight of her body in the semi-nude state.

"The bra..." she said in a rasp. The sound would have been a red warning sign for a more knowledgeable woman.

Krista reached around to take it off, but Ingrid

114

quickly stepped forward. "Let me help!"

The woman's fingers played on Krista's back, much longer than necessary. Then as the fingers reached around to help Krista slip out of the bra, she felt them caress into her breasts. Then the bra was off.

Ingrid stepped around and gazed in fascination at Krista's naked breasts. "They're *beautiful!*" Then, as if she were afraid of being stopped, she stepped forward, saying, "Just let me feel their smoothness!"

Krista finally realized what was happening. Before she could react, the woman's hands were on her breasts, caressing them intimately. Without wanting to, Krista found that she was responding. Her breasts seemed to warm under the touch. As the fingers gently moved across the tips of her breasts, she felt the nipples harden, go erect and rigid.

"Don't!" she objected, afraid now.

"Please—it won't hurt. You'll find it nice. Wonderful!" Ingrid murmured heatedly in a rasping voice. "Only a woman really knows how to caress another woman to desire and passion. Only a woman can really thrill another woman. You don't know what it's like until you have experienced it with a woman. It's different—*more* exciting, more wonderful!"

All the time her fingers were working on Krista, sending mild pleasure through her.

Suddenly she realized how it could be with a woman and felt a stab of confusion.

"What are you talking about?"

"Oh, come on, honey, you aren't all that innocent, are you?"

The woman's eyes feasted on Krista's body as if

she wanted to devour every inch of flesh.

"You are a very lovely woman and—" But the voice trailed off as Ingrid stepped closer.

"I don't know what you are talking about!" Krista announced in a shaking voice. It was a lie she wished to God was true.

Ingrid laughed; suddenly she was leaning down, her lips touching Krista's.

A hand slid along her shoulder, down to the soft supple form of her breast.

For some reason Krista couldn't move.

Then the probing of the woman's tongue suddenly broke the erotic spell that had kept Krista paralyzed. Awareness that her own lips had automatically parted terrified her.

Without actually realizing it, she was relaxing, responding to the fondling touch of the other woman's hand against her breast, the greedy exploration of her mouth.

She was giving in, against her will finding the erotic nearness of the woman pleasant and even exciting in a horrid, revolting, degenerate way.

Then something snapped through her mind— something which cut away all the pleasure that the mere caressing of body on body, hands to breasts had created. She forcefully pushed away from the older woman.

Krista took several steps backward, then cried:

"Don't! Not again! I don't want this kind of thing!" Ingrid Heinisch stood, staring passionately at her, breathing hard. Slowly the wild expression in her eyes seemed to simmer lower and lower; then it faded. Sighing tiredly, the woman dropped her head.

"I'm sorry! Nobody should force another person

into something they don't want. For a moment there, I thought maybe you might like it," she said, defeated.

Krista was dizzy with disgust. She felt sorry for the woman standing before her, and at the same time was inwardly nauseated at what had almost happened. There was a long silence; Miss Heinisch was the first to break it.

"Get dressed! I'll call one of the other girls in— they can train you from here on. You'll have just a few days to shape up. And if you don't, not even Mr. Schmidt could save you! There was anger and bitter hatred in the words—open threat.

Krista had managed to gain control of her own emotions by now and glared at the other woman. "You'd just better be careful yourself!"

"You threatening me?"

"Peter Schmidt wouldn't like what you did to me!"

'I didn't get very far, did I?" was the bitter reply.

"Let's just try to forget it," Krista suggested generously. "*I* don't think that Peter—"

"So it's 'Peter,' is it?" The words were biting and nasty. "Well, now I see it all. You're another one of his sluts!"

Anger welled through Krista, and it was only with conscious control that she managed to refrain from saying anything in reply. Shrugging her shoulders, Krista reached for her clothing, and started getting dressed, while the other woman stomped out of the office to get one of the models.

Krista sighed tiredly, realizing she had made a dangerous enemy in Ingrid Heinisch. This was the kind of enemy she couldn't afford to have.

Chapter Thirteen

The following days were filled with activity for Krista, but none of it included Peter Schmidt. He seemed to disappear completely from her life.

The young girl, Rosewitha, turned out to be a lively coach. She was friendly and warm; a good companion. They had coffee breaks and lunch together.

Krista hardly saw Gisela in the evening, for her roommate was involved in heavy dating which kept her out most of the evening and night.

A couple of times Werner called, and Krista went out with him. When they would end up in his apartment, she found the nights puzzling and yet happily satisfying. She would dream of Peter Schmidt, but it was Werner Pawlík who possessed her body.

In his arms it could be anything from tenderness to harsh carnal orgasm.

One night when they were alone, he turned and looked at her like some beast, said: "Undress!"

But before it was possible to do more than slip out of her skirt, he was at her.

She responded automatically to his brutal mood.

As his hands almost ripped off her panties,

Krista experienced a raw voluptuous thrill.

Brutally he almost threw her onto the bed and swiftly parting her legs, began kissing them with frantic tongue caresses, lips greedily sucking on her flesh.

She lay back on the bed almost shivering from the wild pleasure his lips gave her as they feasted greedily upon her. His hands slipped up under her legs, around and over to her breasts, clawing at the supple flesh.

"Oh, don't!" she almost cried out in pain and pleasure. Then as his tongue lingeringly caressed her, she sobbed, "Yes, oh, yes!"

Her hands clutched at the covers in a desperate need to have something to do.

Then she was embracing his head against her in a climax of sexual pleasure, her hips surging up against the man's voluptuous kisses, legs trembling, every nerve and muscle screaming in orgasm.

Then the man had made slow, careful love to her, caressing her breasts, kissing them, tenderly making over her body as if it were too delicate and might shatter. Such was the man's different moods that Krista didn't know how she felt about his love-making.

Krista found it impossible to really turn the man down, considering his ability to make love in so many different ways that she never knew what would happen next.

One evening, as they were lying on his bed after a prolonged session which had left them momentarily tired, he asked how she was getting along with her work.

"They've been fitting me for dresses. I guess

I'm in." Then she told him about the event with Ingrid Heinisch.

He laughed. "That's just about what to expect. The business is filled with such people. Gerd Richter is one. He only likes men. You'll have to get used to it—unless you might consider getting attached to a man and marrying him."

Werner was thoughtful for a moment, then hesitantly said: "You know, I'm getting quite—well, I'm beginning to like you very much."

"I like you, too, Werner," she told him, hoping desperately that he would leave it there. It was impossible to miss the implication of his words, the setting and timing. Woman's intuition warned her.

For a moment Werner hesitated, then continued, moving a gentle hand across her stomach. It wasn't a sensual action, but rather an intimate tenderness. "There's something about you, Krista, that makes a man think wild thoughts. Wild, I mean, in that maybe they never thought them before. There are many women in the world, and many who give themselves freely to a man; but they have a cheapness about them which leaves no thought—or room for thoughts—of tenderness. You're different. A man can't think of you in any other terms except wanting—physically, emotionally desiring to protect and care for you. Don't ask me why." He broke off, as if having said too much. Then his finger-tips gently moved across her thighs. "A man could want you for a very long time." He laughed nervously. "Look at me! I'm only old enough to be your father—and you've got me romantically involved! I'm not the visual concept of the great lover—not like Peter Schmidt—and I don't have anything but

security to offer a woman. Yet I'd give you everything I have, just for the asking."

His voice was a mixture of light seriousness and
joking. His eyes were deadly serious. It wasn't hard
to realize he was trying to say he loved her and
wanted her, but knew how impossible it all was, and
at the same time trying to make it all sound like a
joke, in case she might laugh at him. A girl didn't
need experience with a man to understand that.

Krista didn't know what to say, and for a long
time the silence was almost depressing.

"Well," Werner stated in a husky voice, drop-
ping. his eyes away from her, taking in the full
sweep of her body, "I'm not a fool. And I know it
will be impossible to hold you much longer—that's
to be expected. A man like me is lucky to have a
woman like you for even a little while. You're the
type that will go far. Gisela saw that, and I saw it.
Peter Schmidt sees it—and he's in a better position
than I am to help you. I only hope you don't get hurt
in the process."

"You're too harsh on yourself," Krista scolded,
forcing a warm, tender smile. Then she had the impulse to be honest with him, to tell Werner a few
thoughts she felt. "At first I didn't find you very—
attractive—but you're the kind of man who's gentle
and sweet—"

"The story of my life!"

"No! I mean it. I've never known anybody like
you before, and I can't help feeling very attracted to
you—"

"And *only* 'attracted'!" Werner said, a little bitterly.

Krista reached out her hand and gently touched

122

his face with her fingertips. "Don't. That's not fair to yourself! You have many qualities that any woman would be glad to have in a husband or lover." Then she smiled teasingly. "And you're a wonderful lover, too!"

"That! That I pride myself on!"

The seriousness had slipped away now, and she was thankful for that. They both laughed, and for a long time neither of them said anything, just gazing into one another's eyes.

"You're a she-devil!" Werner exclaimed, leaning closer to Krista and brushing his lips to hers. For a time they merely kissed, then suddenly the gentleness burst into wild, demanding passion.

Krista found emotions flushing over her as if some tidal wave had washed into the room, drowning all thought and all awareness except that which centered around the man caressing her. She felt his touches as they moved over her body. His fingers softly smoothed the silk of giving breasts, sending ecstatic pleasure whipping through their warmth and their eager hunger for kisses.

The feel of his tongue as it slipped between her lips sent a desperation through her.

Without realizing it, her hands slipped down between them, caressingly.

He rolled over on his back, openly inviting her to do anything she wished.

"You are a very lovely woman!"

"You're a lovely, sexy man."

All at once she couldn't control herself. The feel of his hard flesh, hot and silky burned her to desperate need.

She lifted, pointed the tip and then surged down

upon it, taking in the full length of that hard, thick male rod. Slowly she lifted, almost letting it leave her, only to thrust down. It was thrilling to have so much control over what was happening.

When she lifted again, she slowly circled around and around on the tip.

"Hell, you do that good!" Werner exclaimed in pleasure.

"How's this?" Krista inquired, dipping down to take in all of him, then reached between her legs so that it was possible to rub his testicles.

"Hell, be careful!"

She laughed, replying with: "You'll last! I know!"

But all at once Krista knew she wouldn't last and started pumping up and down faster and faster on him until abruptly the gathering climax like a volcano.

Lava seemed to flow between them and then Krista was lifting away and falling back on the bed.

Werner turned and rested a hand on her breast, saying, "Oh, you can be great! Just great!"

Chapter Fourteen

The next day Peter called Krista into his office.

"I hear you're doing pretty well. The girls say you've caught on fast." He smiled warmly. "I'm glad!"

Peter leaned across the desk and gazed into her eyes. "Think you have time in your dating schedule to see someone interested in knowing you better?"

For a moment Krista didn't know what he was talking about. Then realization jolted through. Happily she answered him. "I believe it *could* be arranged."

"How about tonight?" he offered. "Dinner, the opera. You like opera?"

"I love it—but I've never seen one!" Krista exclaimed with delight.

"Then it's settled." After a moment of silence he looked at her, stood, and said: "Well, we had both better get back to work."

As she started to leave, he called, "I hear you had a run in with Ingrid the other day."

"Oh—"

"Forget it. She's attempted to give me bad reports, but I ignored them, after checking with the other girls. The show is in another week!"

"I've already forgotten it. I feel sorry for her."

"Don't waste your time. She's well settled in her profession and accepts what she is. That's important regardless. Being settled in what you are and accepting it." As an afterthought, he added: "How many of us are so well adjusted?"

Krista thought about that all day, wondering what it was he had been trying to tell her. Finally she gave up trying to figure it out. She was excited about the prospect of having her first date with Peter Schmidt, and realized that possibly she inwardly wanted him to make love to her.

She was about ready to leave for her apartment when a phone call came for her. It was Gisela.

"Krista," the voice said over the phone, filled with tight emotion, as if controlling itself.

"Yes? What's wrong?" She felt inner warning that something had happened which involved her, but what it might be, it was impossible to guess. Only fear iced her nerves; a cold sweat drowned her excitement about the night's promise.

"Your stepfather..." The words were meek and faded. They hesitated.

"What's wrong?" Mixed emotions flooded over her at the mention of Karl Roher.

"He's—killed himself!"

For a moment Krista stood in a daze, not knowing if she felt anything. There had never been any affection in her heart for the man; and after what he had done, she could have killed him herself. But this news stunned her.

"The police want to talk to you about it. He left a note, saying why he killed himself. Telling about the—what he did to you. They called and are on their way over here. They wanted me to get hold of you."

"I'll be right there."

Without another word, Krista hung up the phone. Then she called for a taxi. It seemed as if the emotions had been drained from her; no feeling remained. No thought about Peter Schmidt and the date for the evening, or telling the man that it would now be impossible. She only thought about that last night with her stepfather and the hate which she felt for him, and wondered why it wasn't possible to hate him now.

Ten minutes later she was getting into a cab, giving directions to her apartment.

* * * * * * *

The note read:

>   "I can't live with myself any longer. What I did in a fit of drunken passion to the daughter of my dead wife has left me with deep guilt feelings which I find it impossible to live with. I want to see Krista and tell her how horrible I feel—tell her that I regret the terrible sexual act I committed. The only excuse is a simple man's uncontrollable loneliness and hunger for a young girl who lived with him.
>   "Yet I realize that she would not understand or forgive, or even listen to my words.
>   "Each day dragged on my mind;

each night was filled with the self dis-
gust of what I'd done to poor little
Krista. And now there is nothing to live
for. Life has been hard for me. Maybe
the war and all the things which went
on before and after are the reason that
a man can become such an animal, los-
ing all sense of right and wrong. I've
tried to tell myself that these were to
blame, and not myself: Yet I was finally
forced to face the fact that a person can
never put blame on someone or some-
thing else for his actions. Our nation
has done this much—too much in the
last years—blamed others for our
faults. I'm tired of it all. The only an-
swer is death.

"Karl Roher."

Krista looked up from the handwritten letter and
into the eyes of the hardened police officer.

"Why didn't you report what he did?" the man
demanded.

Krista felt emotion and a deep pity for Karl Roher, which surprised her. Yet that note had held the
longing and guilt and the torment of a very unhappy
man—a man whom her mother had loved and married.

She managed to choke out: "I didn't think it
necessary."

Gisela quickly spoke up for her. "Krista was in a
terrible state when she came here that night. We
never talked about it, but I believe it was because

enough pain had come from what the man did to her. She wanted to forget, not bring it up again and again. You can't blame her."

"A full report will have to be made, and you'll have to sign it," the man told Krista in a tight, authoritative voice.

Suddenly she wanted to cry; break down and cry out all the agony and all the pain which that experience had brought her and which today's event had returned to her mind. It was only with forced control that she remained outwardly calm.

"I'll do whatever you want, but can I get it done tomorrow?"

The man nodded. Then, after telling her where to report, he turned and ordered the other two men to leave with him.

Gisela quickly asked, before they left, "You won't let this get into the papers?"

The officer turned. "I can't promise anything."

"You can keep her name—"

"I'll do my best," he promised, shrugging his shoulders. Then he turned and left.

When the door closed, Krista's reserve and emotional restraint shattered. Turning toward Gisela, she felt tears streaming down her cheeks as a sob choked in her throat.

The other woman rushed to Krista's side and put her arms around her. "Go ahead—it might help!"

For several minutes she cried, unable to control herself.

Gisela gave her a strong brandy a few minutes later, and control settled over her nerves with the effects of the liquor. They sat on the green sofa, each quietly involved with her own thoughts. Krista didn't know how much time passed before there was a knock on the front door.

Instant remembrance jarred her into action. "Oh, God, that must be Peter Schmidt!"

"What?" Gisela cried.

"I have a date with him. I can't, just can't go out, now!"

Gisela shook her head. "No—you go! I'll stall him while you get ready. It'll do you good!"

"Oh, I can't!" Krista pleaded, desperate.

"Don't be foolish. You can't walk out on a date with a man like him! You might not get another chance. And I promise it'll be good for you! Go into the bedroom and get ready!"

Gisela pushed Krista toward the bedroom and shouted toward the front door, "Be right there!" Then she whispered to Krista. "Hurry! Rush!"

Resignedly Krista moved toward the bedroom.

Chapter Fifteen

Dinner and drinks helped. The opera was a production of Puccini's *La Bohème,* and its story and music had cast a romantic mood over her, fading away the earlier depression. As they drove in Peter Schmidt's silver Mercedes, she didn't want the evening to end.

"It's been wonderful," Krista told him, leaning closer to the man. It was impossible to get near enough to Peter because of the sports car's shift, which was centered between the seats.

"Past tense?" he asked, smiling, turning his eyes in her direction for a brief moment.

She recovered quickly, laughing. "Is, then! It's wonderful! You don't know how much I've wanted to go out with you!"

He merely smiled and was silent for a little while.

"Where are you taking me now?" Krista asked, feeling she knew.

"Thought you might like a little dancing."

"Oh," she started to say, disappointed. Then she added, "On second thought, that sounds wonderful!"

"Sounds like you had something else in mind?"

"Never can tell," she countered lightly.

They were silent until he had brought the car to a stop, parking it on the street. Peter got out, rushed around to the other side, and helped her. They walked to a small club which bore the name *Mocombo*. Peter was quickly recognized and taken to a choice table in a dimly lighted corner which afforded them the best privacy the place had to offer, along with a good view of the dance floor and the small combo.

"I come here often," Peter told her, taking hold of her hand.

"So I noticed," she replied. "I bet you bring all your women here."

Peter raised his eyebrows. "What makes you think I have *that* many girls?"

"Oh..."

"Oh, nothing! You shouldn't even mention such a thing. It's not nice."

"Isn't it? Shouldn't a woman be interested in what kind of a man she goes out with?"

'What's that got to do with other women?"

"Well, a man takes a lot of women out and all of them to the same place, well..."

"You imply I'm a rake."

"Aren't you?" she smiled, squeezing his large hand.

He hesitated, then admitted, "Maybe I am—but I don't believe in just running from one woman to another. I keep to one at a time."

"That's nice of you," Krista said bitingly.

"I think so. Anyway, I don't devour women the way my reputation would make people think. To me, a woman is something special, and each deserves a different kind of attention. And nobody in

132

their right mind is bed-hopping from one to another. One woman is enough for any man to handle!"

"Oh, now you think you can handle women?" Krista teased.

"At least most of them make me think so," he laughed.

The waiter came up then, and they ordered drinks. Krista surprised him by asking for a martini.

"I see Werner has gotten to you more than I thought!" he scolded, when the man had left.

"What in the world makes you think that?"

"The martini. Not many drink cocktails like that. It takes a particular taste—"

"Werner is a nice man."

"How nice?"

"Now who's prying? I thought it wasn't proper to talk about other women; the same should apply to other men."

"Why?"

"Because—just because. You don't want to know what happens when I'm with another man, do you?"

"Don't I? Might be revealing!"

"You need a road map to know how to handle a woman?" Krista demanded.

Peter laughed delightedly. "Very good! You had the last word!"

"A woman should always get the last word, don't you think?"

"That depends on the woman," he answered evasively.

"Oh?"

The conversation lagged for awhile. After the drinks had come and the combo started playing romantic dance music, Peter suggested a dance.

The movement of his body against hers as they danced excited every dream and every expectation she had felt the man would inspire. It was like dancing with a Greek God who had come from some fantasy. His body was as hard and strong as she had imagined it to be. He was one of the few men who lived up to the advertisement.

It seemed as if they were having respectable intercourse on the dance floor, without anybody being able to notice. She found it almost impossible not to whisper a suggestion in his ear that they go someplace to be alone. Only the knowledge that this was his duty, not hers, prevented the request. She kept her desire a secret, and hoped he would bring it out into the open by a request of his own.

When the music finally stopped and the combo took a short break, they stepped up to their table and sat silently, sipping their drinks.

"You dance nicely," she told him.

"So do you."

The silence was oppressive and awkward, moving between them like some alien thing attempting to build a wall to block communication. Krista thought he would never break it.

"Want to go?" he asked. The way Peter said it made Krista tense, startled. It wasn't merely a suggestion that they leave, but also a statement of where he intended to take her.

Ten minutes later they were driving quietly through the streets of Hanover. The moonlight shone over the world, casting a brightness on Peter's features, lending them a soft, glowing outline. The desire to lean close and kiss his cheek was almost overwhelming. She desperately wanted to feel him near, to be aware of his strength, to gain the intimate knowledge which only lovers discover about one another.

Peter didn't say anything; he didn't have to. Both of them knew where they would go, and what would follow. When he pulled up to a large, modern, expensive looking apartment house and headed the car into the garage, there was no need for explanation. He merely said, "This is where I live."

They got out of the car and silently went into the building, walked to an elevator and waited. A few moments later they were on the top floor of the building, moving down a hallway.

"I've rented a rather nice place, I think. Hope you like it." The quality of his voice told her more than words could have. He was honestly interested in her reaction to his place; almost as if he desired her approval, as if it might be important to him— very important.

He opened his door, stepped back, and let her enter first.

Krista was startled and wide eyed at what she saw. It was almost like a movie set. Never had she seen such luxury. If Werner's and Gerd Richter's place had seemed expensive, this was like a dream palace.

A huge bay window on the far wall overlooked the city, giving a view which she had never seen before. When Peter turned on the lights, Krista was even more amazed. Bookcases lined one wall; there was actually a real fireplace on the opposite side of the room. This was the perfect bachelor's quarters, from a dream book. The furnishings were low and simple in design, colored off-white. Pull-down lamps were suspended from the high ceiling.

"This is wonderful!" she exclaimed.

"You *really* like it?" he asked boyishly.

"*Like* it? I *love* it!" Krista cried. "Who wouldn't?"

"Well, you never can tell. A lot of my—some of the women I've known in the past didn't think much of it. Thought it a little too—something, but they wouldn't say what!" He laughed and crossed the room. "I'll fix us something to drink, put a fire in the fireplace, then we'll turn the lights down to romantic-dim. How's that?"

"*Wonderful!*" Krista walked over to the fireplace. Above it hung a huge oil painting of Peter Schmidt. She gazed at it for a long time and was startled when the man came up behind her.

"Here's some brandy. Thought that might warm us up a little, while I get the fire going."

As he started the fire, Krista sat down in front of it, waiting, sipping the brandy. It warmed her blood, and tasted much better than any she had had before.

Finally Peter sat down beside Krista, his hand just touching hers. He had turned the lights down. Only the moonlight shining through the windows, and the fire itself, gave any outlines to their features.

"I like the quiet. You can almost believe you're in a mountain cabin," he softly told her.

"You're romantic soul, aren't you?"

"I guess so. An idealistic romantic. I've been looking for the golden rainbow of life, and, well, I've never found it. But I keep looking. It's not in business. Sometimes one thinks they find it in a woman, but it doesn't last."

"Oh?"

"I mean, well, a man wants a woman who looks upon him as something important, and looks at their relationship as something beautiful and lovely. I don't know—most of the women I meet are hardened by life, by the world they're in." He hesitated. "That's what makes you different. You still retain your innocent attitude and appearance. You haven't been spoiled."

"Now you're giving me a line," Krista told him, looking over the rim of her glass into his eyes.

"Believe what you will."

"What does that mean?"

"Just that you can't convince a woman you're telling the truth. The harder you try, the worse it gets, so it's better to say nothing. Just leave your words there for the woman to take as she wishes."

Krista was beginning to understand something about the man next to her. Sadness welled in her—a tender, gentle sadness that such a man, with more money and power than any one person needed to be successful and happy, should be lonely and a little lost in the world he moved in.

"It's that hard up there?" she asked.

"Where? Up where? I'm right here beside you."

"And we're a million miles apart," she commented, half to herself.

"Why do you say that?"

"Well, I'm a nobody girl, and—"

"You're Krista Gustav. That's what you told me!"

"But then you asked, 'Who is Krista Gustav?' And I realize she is a nothing—just a young girl trying to make a place for herself in the world. And you're the giant—the king—the prince with princely riches and power, bringing this innocent into your castle, showing her around, amazing her, creating within her a deep awe and respect for the wonders of your world, knowing how far away they are from her own existence and world."

"Child, you are crazy in the head!" he laughed, patting her cheek.

The intimate tenderness of his touch fired something within each of them, and for a long moment they were silent, gazing deep into one another's eyes. The gap between their worlds seemed suddenly to close, as if it didn't matter, didn't mean anything, and the doubts which had seeded within Krista's mind seemed to melt away; the dream of having her prince make her his princess seemed almost a possible reality.

"You *are* beautiful," he murmured in a husky voice.

"I thought I was before," was Krista's answer. The words were light and teasing, but her voice was serious and soft, as if waiting breathlessly for that moment when their lips would meet. The words were nothing; they had no effect on the mood, they had no power over what was slowly happening.

"You were beautiful the first night I saw you— something rang in my heart, something became music and began a song which had no words, but held all the meaning of all the words in all the languages in the world which concern love and romance and tenderness and those emotions which man feels for woman. And that has been playing over and over, every time I think of you, every time I see—"

Suddenly he wasn't saying anything, for their

lips had met. Met with such tenderness that Krista was breathless, even spellbound. A gentle wildness burned through her at the birth of that kiss, mixed with the soft touch of love and deep longing of one lonely searching heart reaching desperately and openly toward another.

They didn't attempt more; they didn't try to make the perfection of that kiss anything other than what it was—a reaching out, a touching of hearts.

He slid away, and they were silent for a long time, gazing blindly into the fireplace.

Then, without warning, Peter turned and grabbed Krista, folding his arms around her body. Their lips met, this time with breathtaking violence and demanding fire. She felt herself crushed against his body, and that wildness fired every nerve and cell, burning, searing, furiously overwhelming.

They embraced with every inch of their bodies, stretching out on the floor. Their tongues ran rhythmically at one another, driving a frantic passion through them. She felt her breath gasping, tightening, and choking her lungs. She was aware of the trembling of every muscle, helpless, overcome—trembling that had never been there before, trembling that seemed to reach down to her soul.

It was impossible to believe that anything could be this good. Peter was so different from what she'd expected.

Sex had become a part of her life; a kind of sex that could have an element of tenderness and maybe affection because it gave such pleasure.

But nothing like this.

Where before there were limits she might have regarding what it was possible to let a man do to her, now she realized that with the right man there wasn't anything she wouldn't and couldn't do.

It was a helpless state of mind that made her resistance to any possible demands nonexistent.

She could feel the manly hardness of Peter like some Greek God. It wasn't pure carnal desire. This was something that went far below the surface.

How she wanted to feel him against her lips, but in a loving, giving way. All she could think of was giving as much pleasure as possible to this man. Before, with the other experiences, it had been more experimental than real. This time, Krista realized, it would be far different.

Her mind screamed: *What's happening to me?*

Yet she was quite certain that deep down there wasn't any mystery to the answer. Sex was one thing; being loved and loving was totally different.

"God! What's come over me?" Peter cried as they broke for breath. He searched her eyes. "I've never experienced such a thing. Never before."

There was no cause for further comment; nothing more could be said with words. This was the silent communication of two lovers, needing no words and no expression except the exchange of glances, the nearness, and the tender touch.

They lay there for awhile, then Peter gathered Krista up in his arms and carried her into the bedroom. Her eyes were tightly shut, waiting for her lover's lips, his love kisses, and his caresses.

She felt those strong hands gliding over her body; she was aware of clothing blending away into the darkness. She helped him. No words were needed, nothing but the awareness of Peter Schmidt being so intimately near. His hands loved her body.

His lips followed his hands, covering all her clothing, caressing her like soft, light silk. The warmth gently began to build, carefully adding to the desire, the hunger to be one with her man.

She was discovering love for the first time!

"Oh, Peter," she murmured in delight and pleasure as his hands caressed across her body. She was never aware of when or how he removed he clothing, only became aware of the fact that he was caressing her naked flesh. It was as if by magic he had made her suddenly naked to his loving caresses.

There wasn't anything vulgar about his touch or actions. He was loving her with caresses as no man had done before.

Yet the actions were much the same.

She trembled as his hand touched her thighs, passed across them, lingered between them for a moment of discovery.

She lifted up so that the feel of his touch would center on the most sensitive nerves of her flesh.

A wave of deep pleasure welled through Krista as his fingers slid into her very being and then along the flat of her stomach and finally across the points of her breasts. Then he was touching her cheek.

She turned and moved against Peter, thrilling to the body contact.

Their lips met, open, tongues thrusting eagerly together. The kiss was erotic but filled with so much emotional meaning that it left Krista dizzy.

When the kiss parted, Peter gently urged her back onto the bed and then lowered his lips along her throat, down across her shoulder and finally into the fullness of one breast.

"Oh, how you do it!" she sighed, lifting up

against his parted lips, thrilling to the tongue kisses he gave her nipple.

This was like nothing she had ever experienced before.

Why that should be so, Krista couldn't really fully understand. Why should one man's simple kisses mean so much? Why should they do so much to her in a physical-sexual way?

Then he was burying his lips against her stomach, lovingly sucking, caressing with mouth and tongue, exploring her navel, then slowly lowering.

She embraced his head, caressing the back of his neck with tender fingers, wanting to give him some sensation of the pleasure his love-making waved through her.

"Oh, Peter, love me so beautifully!" she said, knowing it didn't make sense, yet wanting to somehow express the feelings welling deep within her. "Oh, you are beautiful!"

Then his lips lowered, inching to her thighs, crossing the aching swell of her, lightly touching and flitting away, slowly returning after worshipping her thighs. She surged up against his kiss and he penetrated her in such an erotic manner that Krista felt as if she were near climax.

"Don't wait, please!" she pleaded.

But he gripped her to him, showering her with tender, passionate kisses that drove every nerve tighter towards orgasm.

The world spun, seemed to close in upon her consciousness, squeeze to a pin-point of sensation too beautiful to bear.

She clutched her fingers into his hair, caressed down along his muscular steel shoulders as a convulsion whipped through to climax.

Then Krista became aware of the man touching, kissing; tonguing her breasts, moving gently from one to the other.

Love-words sounded from his mouth, yet she couldn't understand them. It seemed as if all sensation were centered upon the pleasure of his body. Sound was only a distant melody.

Then Krista parted her thighs and he moved upwards, almost, but not entering her depths; only lovingly touching, waiting, aware of what would happen soon enough but willing to wait in order to experience every beautiful moment as if it were a total climax in itself.

When they finally did move it was a slowly lingering joining surge that united them in a total partnership. It was more than physical penetration; it was literally like becoming one being.

The gathering tenseness of pleasure surged through her as he finally rested deeply within her.

Neither moved for a moment, for each of them wanted to experience the pleasure of knowing the first seconds of their total union.

Her mind kept screaming over and over that she was possessing him completely. Finally, at last. He was hers, totally. And the knowledge of that was overwhelming.

"Oh, Peter, you are wonderful!" she almost sobbed, looking up into his eyes.

The expression on his face was that of a man bathed in complete pleasure.

"You're so beautiful, Krista," he told her.

Then his hips moved and she experienced the joy of the man deeply possessing her in a total act of passion and love.

Every penetration was impressed upon her conscious awareness so strongly that she was able to experience every instant of pleasure as if it were in itself an eternity.

As climax gathered, her legs tensed about his, her whole body seemed to coil about the man that penetrated her so deeply. From that moment on she lived in a fantastic world of sensation, a continual series of lovely, wonderful waves of pleasure that mounted higher and higher until she felt so dazed and so completely surrounded by the endless joy that reached deep into her very soul that she thought it would last forever. She surely never wanted it to end; to come to some kind of vulgar climax. Yet the mounting ecstasy that surrounded her very being, her universe, was beyond control. Then the world spun in such a fury of sensation that by the time it had throbbed away, awareness seemed distant. She floated down through a strange universe which had never been a part of her life until this night in her lover's arms. She never wanted it to end. She needed it to continue. Every nerve in her hungered to know those sensations this wonderful man had created.

It was some time before she was willing to face reality; to accept that the ecstasy had washed slowly away. The room was alive around her, dark, silent, but alive with something which had never existed before.

She knew that Peter lay next to her, now. She knew that it wasn't a dream.

Krista bathed in this aftermath for a long time, not certain if sleep had gathered about her thoughts or not.

Then awareness pinpointed when she heard Peter's voice whisper softly near her.

"You are so beautiful," he said.

Then a gentle hand caressed her. The touch sparked swift desire. Immediately she wanted this man to possess her once again. And knew at the same time it was his desire, too.

"Peter, oh, Peter," she breathed against his lips a moment before they kissed one another.

When she thrust her tongue past his teeth, he gently tugged it deeper, pressing it against the roof of his mouth.

He drew her tighter to him and she was aware of his own excitement already highly charged. Then he started making love to her once more.

It seemed as if she were being bathed with an endless liquid of pleasure and touches and sensations. As if he could never get his fill of moving over her form with his lips and hands.

The passion didn't reach overwhelming proportions at first. Instead, it began gently building, then relaxing, building and relaxing, as if her physical desires were on a lightly moving ocean, with soothing breezes making the surface rise and fall.

The pleasure of his touch never tired, never lessened, never weakened. It built slowly, becoming by degrees more and more hungry, more wanting of such beauty. For this was beauty without end— beauty which defied her understanding, her ability to even attempt to comprehend.

Then, without knowing when, his hands became more intimate in their searching. They were forceful, more animated now, finding places they hadn't discovered before, awakening feelings which she had never felt before. This was a concerto of love which was arriving at the last movement, building toward the climax with a slow pulsing beat, a slow progressive tension.

Yet never did the tenderness leave his hands; never did the gentleness escape his kissing and caressing lips as they searched over the velvet of her skin. Never once did the man lose the mood or melody of his musical rapture of love.

And then the final movement reached its summit, its climaxing last moments. Krista found herself being whipped through all the savage wildness, the frantic passion, and the desperate thrashing movement which at last joined their bodies in the final rhythms. The melody, which seemed to have been playing for an eternity throughout the whole perfection of the man's lovemaking, was still strong, still as lilting, still as lovely and beautiful. Even in those last frantic seconds when ecstasy made her lips moan and her whole insides erupt with unbearable pleasure, Krista never once lost the final theme which his hands and lips, and finally his body, had played.

Then she found herself drifting on a soft blackness. Drifting downwards into an opening pit which finally engulfed all consciousness, all awareness except that of the man who was still clinging gently to her as they fell together into the exhaustion of spent-out sleep.

Chapter Sixteen

The next day Peter drove Krista back to the apartment she shared with Gisela. He said little, and there was that about his mood which alarmed her. Almost as if he didn't *want* to talk; as if it were finished or something had gone wrong, or that having possessed her, he wasn't interested any more. Peter was moody, and seemed almost angry.

It wasn't until later in the morning that she arrived at work, having had to report to the Police Station. During that time an inner fear had kept raging inside Krista; she was afraid they might make trouble for her for not having reported the rape. However, everything went smoothly. She signed the reports, then left.

Ingrid Heinisch made a biting comment about her late appearance. "We don't have everything running around you, Krista! You can't come in late—"

"I told *Peter* about it! He said it would be all right!" Krista's retort accented the fact that she had used tile man's first name.

There was a mild murmur from the other models, and Ingrid Heinisch cursed under her breath and dropped the subject.

All that day, Krista expected a call from Peter. The silence was oppressive. By the time she returned home in the evening, there was no doubt in her mind that Peter Schmidt had handed her one of the best, most smoothly perfected lines a man ever gave. The line hadn't merely been of words, but of actions and moods. It didn't seem possible that it could have been an act, yet the silence seemed to indicate the truth of this.

Gisela wasn't home that evening, and the loneliness was heavy on Krista. She wanted to be with Peter; she wanted to be held in his arms, to know him once more as she had the night before. But there wasn't any Peter this time—only her loneliness. In her depressed mood she would have welcomed Werner, merely as a means of escape.

Cigarettes filled the ashtrays. She attempted to read, but found no pleasure or interest in the printed words.

Finally there was only liquor to turn to. Desperately she drank several shots of brandy, then got undressed and slipped into bed.

For a long time Krista lay there, unable to relax, unable to think of anything except Peter Schmidt and the dream that had become reality the night before.

What had been a fantasy, a fascination on her first meeting and all those which had followed, had turned into something real and strong and demanding while in his arms. He was more than a mere "prince" from a fairy story. He was a man who had kissed her, a lover who had the power and skill of long practice in the arts of love.

Why hadn't he called? What had gone wrong?

Would she ever be in his arms again, know the perfection again?

For more than an hour the pain and anguish tormented her, until she thought it would be impossible to stand it any longer. Getting up and having another double shot of brandy to calm her nerves, she again attempted to find rest. It came with the effects of the liquor, but it was a tossing, restless sleep, plagued with haunting dreams.

She found herself in a dark world, running through a tangled jungle, vainly attempting to find her way to the "castle of Peter Schmidt." She caught sight of it through the mass of trees, but never reached it, never found her dream lover. When she awoke in the morning, a thin layer of sweat covered her body.

Chapter Seventeen

In the next days, no word came from Peter. Krista came to the point where she thought her nerves would break. Each night it was necessary to drink more brandy in order to calm herself to sleep; and each sleep was tormented more and more with nightmare dreams of searching for Peter Schmidt through the dark jungle of horror.

The final fittings of the dresses for the fashion show were being made, and the strain at work was pressing at her on every side.

When Werner called one afternoon, asking if she wanted to go out that evening, Krista could have jumped through the phone line and kissed him right then. Never had she been so glad to hear from a man in her life.

That evening he picked her up at work and they went out to dinner. The conversation was light until Werner happened to mention Peter Schmidt.

"How are you getting along with your new boss?" he asked casually, taking a bite *of Rebrucken.*

The mention of Peter chilled Krista, and it was impossible to hide the reaction. Her eyes dropped, and a hardness set in her face. For a moment emotion started to dig at her, and then she controlled it.

"What's wrong?" Werner demanded, concerned.

"Oh, nothing. Something I just thought about." It was lame. He dropped the subject. There wasn't any doubt that he had realized the truth. The rest of the dinner was finished in a mild form of polite conversation. After dinner he offered her drinks, and Krista willingly accepted.

It was late before they arrived at his apartment. During the evening he suggested they might go there, his offer was hesitant, as if he expected her to reject it. This was what she had been waiting for—complete escape in a man's caresses and body.

She didn't want to think about the loneliness.

As usual, there weren't any overtures. They went to the bedroom. Werner seemed to have guessed what she wanted.

He took her in his arms. His kiss was filled with affection and tenderness; there was a longing desperation to the embrace. Krista realized how much he must really care for her, how deep his feelings must be.

Then passion welled up in her; demanding, wild. The madness of animal lust; insanity to find this escape.

Her hips ground into his. Her lips parted, her tongue whipped out. She pressed her breasts against his chest.

A gasp broke from her mouth as she felt the strong reaction in the man. He crushed her; he met her violence with his own. This wasn't love or tenderness; this was lust in wild, savage force. Where the night with Peter had been a concerto of love, this was a concerto in violence.

They broke away, and Krista found pleasure in slowly slipping out of her dress, flaunting herself before him. Slowly, one at a time, she edged her breasts from her bra. The man stared as she stripped before him. The desire was stamped on his face like neon lights. Sweat broke from his forehead.

Krista placed her fingers under the elastic of her panties and edged it downwards, carefully teasingly. Her hips rolled and squirmed, and finally they were free of the restraining clothing. She stood defiantly before him, stark naked, finding a voluptuous thrill at the sight of the anxiety on the man's face.

Werner gaped at Krista, then quickly started undressing.

The roundness of his body, the flabbiness, momentarily reminded Krista of how hard and smooth, how perfect Peter Schmidt had been—and what a bastard.

She had to accept the man was not going to be an important part of her life—at least not an intimate one.

The future, apparently, would be filled with men like Werner, and she might as well get used to that reality. Life was hard; love could be difficult to discover; sex an easy thing to get; and survival was all that counted.

And she was a survivor!

Chapter Eighteen

As the days passed, Krista found the exhaustion of preparing for the fashion show taking up most of her thoughts and time. When she returned to the apartment, what energy was left had little room for thoughts concerning Peter Schmidt. Hate had re-placed the deep love Krista had believed she felt for the man; but she had managed to smother all that; she was now emotionally cold. A wall had built around her feelings.

A couple of times she saw Werner Pawlík, and they went to his apartment for the night. Yet there was little pleasure in the relationship, except a purely physical release.

The days with fittings.

The nights with loneliness.

Or Werner.

They blended, becoming a series of actions she played out, for there was little else left to do.

This was a game of life; it was necessary to go through it until the time of waiting was over.

What she was waiting for, Krista didn't exactly know. She had lost interest in finding out; lost all strength to search.

She drank at night. And somehow had managed

to avoid any hangover. A part of her mind was still focused on the necessity of succeeding. That was her only sane control—and it monitored what she did off-hours.

Then finally the day approached. The moment she had been waiting for; the breath in time toward which all the effort and agony of the past weeks had been building.

The fashion show.

She had to be sharp for the show.

This was her first appearance in public as a fashion model; her first appearance in original designs created under the promotion of Peter Schmidt's company and designed to be exported all over the world.

Her nerves were beginning to suffer. The last days of holding back all feeling, of pressing down all emotions so that she could face each moment, each hour, each new day, had drained her strength. And the night before she drank just one brandy, just enough to make her sleepy

Now she was in the dressing room with the other models, putting on an original dress which was priced at 1,500 DM.

It was a gown of shimmering white silk which covered her body in tight folds, accenting every curve and displaying the perfection of her form. It was a dress which Peter Schmidt had instructed Ingrid Heinisch to have Krista wear. The neckline was cut low, but not daringly so; just enough to reveal her shape without being cheap or common. The dress had a certain class, and it gave her the appearance of some movie princess or queen of royalty.

And, of course, it was the dress which they were

selling; not Krista!

When she saw herself in the mirror, Krista was amazed at how wonderful she looked. Never had her figure been more beautifully clothed. Her hair was piled high on her head and had been flecked with silver, giving it a starry effect.

Ingrid Heinisch was almost like a wild woman, shouting orders, giving directions to the girls, jumping nervously from one to another and making last minute adjustments.

The strain fluttered in Krista's stomach. She needed another drink. She wanted to run, to escape; yet at the same time she could hardly wait until she was walking along the platform, in front of the fifty men and women of the fashion world who would see what she and the other eleven models would be showing.

"Krista, don't forget to stand straight!" Miss Heinisch ordered. "And if you—just make one mistake…dearie—you're new and don't get nervous—because—well, you know all that!" And the woman was off to shout at another girl.

As Krista stood and waited to be sent outside into the show room, she told herself there wasn't any reason to be scared or nervous.

This is just a routine showing! her mind said. *It's not as if you were some starlet, or an actress on her opening night. Nobody will even notice you. It's the dress they're interested in—not you!*

Yet the nervousness was there. It was cramping into her guts, causing cold sweat to ice over her body.

What are you doing here, Krista Gustav? What are you trying to prove?

She swayed dizzily.

Rosewitha caught her. "Hey, what's wrong?"

Krista tried to smile, but failed.

"You look pale. Want to sit down?" Concern showed on the girl's face.

Krista shook her head slowly from side to side. "I'll be all right. Just nerves."

But will you?

"Sure you will. All of us are a little jittery—especially the first time!" Rosewitha smiled and patted Krista's arm.

"Okay, girls!" It was Miss Heinisch's voice. "You're on. Get in line, and move out when I tell you."

Time seemed to push at Krista. It blurred. Her vision darkened.

"Okay, Hannelore—you're first!"

The large woman at the head of the line stepped forward through the gray curtains.

There was a murmuring from outside.

A pause.

"Brigitte!" Miss Heinisch whispered, tapping a redhead.

Murmuring. Sighing. Muffled conversation.

"Rosewitha."

"Marianne."

"Krista."

She didn't recognize her name. It was merely a sound in the background.

"*Krista!*" This time it was spoken harshly.

She couldn't move; she just stood there, paralyzed, terrified.

What if she slipped? Stumbled? Fell!

In front of all those people.

"Krista Gustav!" Miss Heinisch ordered. The voice was at her ear, insistent, demanding, angry. *"Get out there!"*

Krista was moving forward. She didn't know her feet were walking; she wasn't aware of anything but terror—that horrible, illogical terror which had no rational meaning, no purpose.

The curtains blinded her and then disappeared.

Krista felt her stomach churning. It seemed as if the world were closing in around her: all her experiences, all the things which had happened in the past weeks, starting with Karl Roher and now climaxing at this moment. Those hours with Werner Pawlík; his words of love and wanting. The lies of Peter Schmidt.

Peter! Oh, Peter! Why? Why did you lie to me? her mind screamed.

She was walking out onto the stage, going through the motions which days and days of practice had perfected.

Pausing.

Turning.

Pausing.

Moving down the ramp to give a better view of the white silk dress which clung to the curves of her body in such a display of beauty that a low murmur sounded as she moved. The dress rustled.

Where was Peter now? What was he doing? What was he thinking?

Suddenly, emotions welled in her which had been crammed down into the depths of her mind for the last days: emotions that had been created in the arms of Peter Schmidt and were so powerful and overwhelming, filled with so much love and passion, that they choked in the tightness of her throat. Her lungs seemed to expand with effort against the tightness of the dress.

Help! Help me, someone!

The world seemed to close in on Krista; squeeze around her.

Who is Krista Gustav?

Where is she going?

What is she doing here? What does she want out of life?

The vision of Peter Schmidt focused before her. The handsome, even features, the dark eyes, the black hair, the strength. Staring at her with desire, with longing, with hunger, and something else.

Suddenly Krista realized that she was looking directly at him. At the real Peter Schmidt. He was sitting at a table with two other men, staring up at her. His mouth was parted in amazement, and his eyes held a strange expression. His face tensed with struggle. Then...

Everything blurred.

Everything was running together.

Faces were flashing before Krista's eyes Movement.

Voices shouting. Screaming after her.

Krista didn't know she was running, didn't even know what she was doing. She wasn't aware of anything.

This was a nightmare

More terrible than anything she had dreamed, more horrible than anything she could have imagined She was swimming in it—in a reality of emotional terror, of overwhelming agony which she just couldn't understand, couldn't control, couldn't stop.

She was running, rushing from the room and down the brightly lighted hallway. Running away from something too painful to face, too tormenting to stand any longer.

Run—get away find escape find yourself—find something—anything but what's in that room!

Krista was rushing into the street, running down the busy sidewalk. People turned to stare after her. She kept running.

She stumbled and fell.

The dress tore. She heard the ripping. She ran again.

A scream broke from her lips, and tears were rushing down her cheeks. The pit of her stomach felt like ice and fire, all mixed together.

"Watch out!" a voice shouted.

Someone bumped against her. She stumbled, then caught her balance. The dress ripped again, but she didn't care. She didn't care about anything.

How long she ran, how long she tried to escape that panic pulsing through her, Krista didn't know.

The world was dark now.

It was night. The streets were filled with night sounds. She was wandering in a familiar section of town, but couldn't, at first, recognize it.

What have you done, Krista? she demanded, saner now, calmer.

It was several moments before Krista realized where she was. It was where Karl Roher and her mother had lived; where she had lived for so many years. For a long time Krista stood in front of the apartment house that had been her home.

You've come a long, long way from here, Krista. A very long way. But do you know what you want, where you are going? What does the future hold with nothing left—nothing to live for, nothing to keep going on for?

Death might be pleasant now. With death would come rest, escape from the pain, escape from the agony of living and struggling and trying to find happiness, for there is no happiness in life. Where could a person find it?

"You look at your life—you want happiness, and it's not on the outside—only inside yourself, only then will you find real contentment!"

But there wasn't anything inside Krista, for without knowing what she was, how could she know what was inside her worthy of being happy for? Death? Was that the answer?

Krista suddenly wanted to be with somebody— anybody. Not to be alone, because she was afraid of what she would do. Death might be too tempting as a way out.

Turning, Krista started walking toward the center of town. *It couldn't be more than half an hour's walk,* her mind said.

Krista hadn't gone three blocks before she sighted a taxi and called it, rushing forward. Once inside, she gave Werner Pawlík's address and collapsed in the seat exhausted.

Chapter Nineteen

When they arrived at Werner's apartment, Krista told the taxi driver she didn't have any money, and asked the man to wait for her. He laughed and said he would have to follow her.

The two of them walked up to Werner's room. She knocked.

They waited.

What was taking him so long? she inwardly screamed.

Knocking again, Krista felt the nervous tension jar through her.

What's keeping him?

"Looks like he isn't home." the man told her in a tired, bored voice. "What now, lady?"

"He *has* to be here!" she cried desperately.

What would she do if he wasn't there? She had to be with someone!

An outward calm had settled over her which belied the inner torment bobbling under the surface. It felt as if her nerves had been ground raw; her mind was on a tightrope of tension, about to snap, breaking all restraint.

Knocking once more, Krista held back the anguish grinding through her. If he wasn't there, she would have to return to her apartment and get money to pay the man. But she didn't want to return. She wanted to be with Werner, or any man, just as long as it was someone with whom she could find escape.

"What now, lady?" the driver demanded in a harsh voice. "You've run up a bill, and—"

"You'll have to take me to my place. I have money there."

The driver stared at her, trying to decide whether he could trust her. "All right, let's go. You're costing me money, waiting here."

The drive to her apartment was a study in control. Every nerve in Krista wanted to cry out, scream against the world, against the existence which had made living an agony and a torture. She didn't want to think; had to have some blank-out, some mental rest from thinking about what had happened, thinking about herself and her life, and what the empty future held.

Krista didn't believe it would be possible to start all over. And it wasn't possible for her to face a life of working in an office every day, doing the same things over and over again like some stupid machine.

How far can a person go? she wondered.

Finally the ride was over, and in ten minutes she was alone in her apartment. The one hope—that Gisela might be there—was shattered. She was alone.

What now, Krista?

Where do you turn now? Where do you go?

The room seemed like an alien thing, a monstrous cell, a prison from which escape was mere survival. If she were in here alone for long, Krista was sure it would be impossible to keep from taking her own life. *It* would be impossible to face those hours without anybody to talk to, without anybody to keep her mind off herself.

Quickly rushing into the bedroom, Krista went to the closet and snatched out a dark blue dress. In moments she had changed, made up her face, and gathered her purse.

Get out! Go someplace! Be with people! Find a man—pick one up! she told herself. *Anything except staying in these four walls, thinking about yourself*

Before leaving, she fixed herself a triple shot of brandy. The effects settled over her nerves and momentarily soothed them. By the time Krista had gotten out into the street, she was feeling a little better. Strength to hold down the anguish had come with the drink.

She headed for the first bar.

Chapter Twenty

How long can you go? That was the question that moved through Krista's mind over and over again as she sat beside the man who had started a conversation with her. The bar was cheap. The beer numbed her mind and emotions.

The man's name was Martin something. She hadn't caught the last part of it, and didn't care to.

His hand played along her leg suggestively. There was little subtlety about what he was doing or what he wanted. It was just a matter of time before he suggested they go some place. Moments, now—she was sure of that.

"What's a classy girl like you doing in a cheap place like this?" the man asked as his hand reached under her skirt and touched the bare smoothness of her thigh.

"Why ask that?" she countered hoarsely.

"Just wondering!"

He was silent for awhile, but his hand squeezed into her leg.

Why doesn't he ask me to leave with him? she wondered, desperately wanting to find the sensual blackout his body could offer her.

You've come a long, long way, Krista. From

rape to picking up a man! Maybe...maybe this is where it will all end! Nothing but a slut.

"Why do you think?"

"You wouldn't want to leave, would you?" The question was asked hesitantly, as if he couldn't believe she would go anywhere with him.

Krista thought how strange it was that she didn't even know what he looked like. They had been sitting there for a long time—how long, she didn't know—and not once had she really looked at his face.

Krista faced the man, staring at his features.

He wasn't bad looking. Average. Heavy, but not fat. Stocky might be a better word. His head was a little too large for his body, but the features weren't bad; a little brutish looking. His thinning blonde hair was brushed back.

"What are we waiting for?" she asked. "Let's go!"

A boldness overcame her as they stood. This was an easy escape. Almost too easy.

The man bought a bottle before they left. Then, leading the way, he directed her toward a nearby hotel. It was necessary to rent two rooms, but one was left completely alone. They went into one room and closed the door behind them.

"Drinks first?" he asked.

"I don't care." Krista shrugged her shoulders and started to undress, without any prologue. It didn't matter that this was a stranger, or that there hadn't been any build up. She didn't care what the man thought of her; he would never see her again after this night. He was a *purpose,* a *means;* merely an object which she used. Beyond that, nothing mattered.

The man stared at her, open-mouthed.

Krista's head was spinning in a dizzy well of liquor. The series of drinks which had mixed in her stomach began to blur all things around her. For a moment she swayed, and then gained control. The man didn't even notice. He was watching her figure as it came free of the dress.

"This isn't a professional thing, is it?" Martin demanded, concerned and anger edging his voice.

"No!" was Krista's simple reply, as she started removing her bra. "I just want something real bad, *real* bad!" Her voice was low and husky. "Hard and big!"

The man stared at her breasts, taking in the full largeness of them, watching them as they swayed with the action of her body.

Krista dropped the bra onto the floor and then went to the bed. Lying down, she told him, "I think I could use that drink now."

Martin stood in the middle of the room, the bottle in his hands. After a moment he said, "Yeah, sure. I'll—"

"Let's drink from the bottle!"

"Sure!"

He went to the bed and sat down beside Krista. For a long time neither of them moved.

It seemed, finally, that the last shred of innocence had been torn away from her. Oddly, Krista found it exciting; keenly thrilling. Like the night with Werner when she had used him for total escape. The complete abandonment of all moral thought, of all restraint, all resistance and guilt. Her old personality drowned to the point where it hardly

166

existed.

Yet a meek voice called out through her mind: *how far down can you go?*

The man opened the bottle of cheap rum and extended it toward Krista.

She lifted it to her mouth and gulped.

The rum burned fire into her throat and for a moment it seemed as if the breath would choke away from her lungs and chest. Then, with the second gulp, a numbness came.

"You're some woman!" the man said, leaning down and clamping a crude hand over her breast.

A tremor raced over Krista's body. Her hands dropped the bottle and it clattered onto the floor, spilling its contents.

Neither of them noticed.

The man was crude and animal. This was living in the naked savagery which had no room for caring.

It was like speeding through a dark tunnel of sensation; like driving dangerously through crowded traffic without any thought of survival. They moved and sought each other.

But somehow that voice inside her seemed to gain force, seemed to keep creeping up, calling for her to stop, to return to the sanity of reality, to become part of the actual world.

Krista tried to ignore that small voice inside her mind. She attempted to drive it away. But it came back, each time with more strength, until sudden guilt and doubt settled through her.

Then disgust.

Horror.

Depression.

How long they had been in the room together, Krista didn't know. They reached for one another, and caressed one another. Then suddenly something snapped inside Krista's mind, inside her emotions. The wall of hardness which had formed, shattered, crumbled, fell away to dust, and she was naked of control.

Her soft sobbing stopped the man. He had been kissing her, caressing her body. He lay motionless, then cursed.

The sobbing changed to racking, uncontrollable crying. Krista shook, and covered her face with her hands.

"What the hell!" The man jumped up from the bed. "What the hell?"

Krista didn't answer him.

She doubled up on the bed, drawing her legs up against her breasts. Her mind was caught in a trap of conflict, of confusion, of grief and self-disgust.

This wasn't Krista Gustav!

A cheap slut, picking up men, having sexual relations just for escape.

This wasn't Krista Gustav!

Krista Gustav was a girl with dreams, with ideals, with longings to be loved and cared for and needed and protected. Krista Gustav was a woman who wanted a man to want her, to hold off the pains and agonies of the world, to give her happiness through his love. She screamed inwardly.

Not a tramp!

Not a whore.

Everything in her cried out for love, for tenderness, for the beauty and perfection which Peter Schmidt had given her one evening. She wanted, needed somebody to turn to.

Oh, God, help me! Help me!

"Help me!" she pleaded aloud. "Help me!" But there was no one in the room to answer her.

She was alone.

It was a long time before Krista realized that the man had left. When she did, she stood and walked into the bathroom. Looking into the mirror, she saw a face which had matured a lot and was now lined with self-pity, with hopelessness.

"You have to face life, Krista," she told the image in the mirror. "Life isn't a fairy tale. Life isn't some book to read and put down. It isn't an experience from some author's fancy. It's cold, harsh reality. You have to find yourself; face yourself realistically."

Filled with doubt and concern, she stared at her reflection. Finally she made a decision.

She would have to start over, but in another town, with new friends. A different world.

Krista nodded and almost smiled.

"Yes, that's a good idea. Go to another town, get a job, and try to learn to live with reality. Maybe meet a man and marry him. Take care of his home. Have children, and raise them to face the cold pain of the hard world they will live in."

Krista turned and walked from the bathroom. She gathered up her clothing and dressed, feeling that at last maturity had come to her. And with that new feeling of maturity came an unemotional awareness and acceptance of what she was.

Krista Gustav?

A woman who had experienced a strange series of events which had given her a mature outlook on life; which would give her the strength to face its coldness, its harsh reality, its bitter impersonality.

A woman who would do her duty, and exist, as all other people did.

Peter Schmidt had been only partly right. You find that which gives strength within yourself. But it wasn't happiness. It was cold acceptance of the raw hard reality of the world. There *wasn't* any happiness. There was merely survival and work and effort, and fighting for a mere living and life. You lived and went on because that was the nature of the human being. But you didn't have happiness; you merely had a momentary state of less pain.

"Life is pain, Krista," she assured herself as she left the hotel room. "And you'll just have to get used to it."

She would return to her apartment and pack her few belongings then take the first bus or train out of Hanover. That would be her first step toward another life, a new life. The life of the *real* Krista Gustav.

Chapter Twenty-One

Krista fitted the key into the front door and then opened it. At first she wasn't aware of the lights being on, or that there was anybody in the room. Then she saw Gisela, who rose from the sofa and rushed forward. A man was sitting in the background.

"Where have you been?" Gisela cried, her voice a high pitched screech. "We've been terrified. We thought something had happened to you!"

Krista stared coldly at the other woman. The dead expression in her eyes stopped Gisela a few feet away.

"What's wrong?" her roommate demanded.

For a moment Krista couldn't think of anything to say. Then the words came, slowly, flatly, without emotion.

"I had a lot of thinking to do." She paused, then added: "Would you help me pack?"

"What?"

"I'm leaving."

Gisela stared at her, shocked. "Now? Leaving?"

Her voice revealed all the amazement and disbelief which was mirrored in her face.

"The sooner the better. I have to get away—far away from Hanover!"

A man's voice cut into the conversation. "That's right—*run!* That's what you should do. Run as far as you can, and discover that you can't run from yourself. Learn that no matter where you go, no matter how far you go or what you do or how you try to get away, you'll never escape that thing inside you which you want to hide from!"

It was Peter Schmidt.

Krista swayed. Her insides were like a volcano—bubbling, heated, shocked.

"What are you doing here?" Her hard, tight voice hid the confusion and surprise and excitement she felt on seeing Peter.

He stood and stepped forward. Gisela backed away and disappeared into the bedroom, closing the door.

Krista was alone with Peter.

"You want to run? Go right ahead! That's a good thing to do. Believe me, because I'm an expert on that! I've been running all my life. In a different way than you, maybe, but it amounts to the same thing!" His voice was heated, but beyond that no actual emotion was revealed. His face was set and hard, but his eyes seemed misty.

"What are you doing here?" Krista demanded again, holding down the frantic emotions inside her.

"Waiting for word about you. We've been scared silly. I—" He broke off, then continued: "Want me to help you pack? You can't do it all alone. You'll need some money. Maybe I could loan you some. I'll drive you the train station—if that's what you want."

They were silent, just staring at one another. Krista didn't know what to think or do or believe.

Why should he be here? What concern was it of his? And after what she'd done to his show.

"Where are you going?" Peter asked casually.

"I don't know," she admitted softly. She began to tremble. "I don't know."

"It doesn't matter, does it? You just want to run away. So you won't have to face life. Try to find that rainbow with the gold at its end."

"There isn't any rainbow, and no gold!" she told him bitterly. "It's faded with eternity—wasn't that what you said?"

"Yes," he admitted, gazing deep into her eyes. "But I've discovered something these last few days. I found that rainbow and the golden treasure it holds. I'd been looking in the wrong direction all my life. I found it—but I'm afraid it's too late."

"You're dreaming!" Krista countered harshly. "It doesn't exist!"

"In you it does. I realized that when you walked out onto the stage this afternoon. I knew then that I loved you and that there wasn't anything I could do about it. That evening we spent together terrified me. I'd never experienced anything like it before. I was afraid of it—and you. So I tried to forget you, tried to ignore you and block you out of my mind, it wasn't possible."

Suddenly everything seemed changed, everything began to glow, exploding into color and bursting, around Krista, overwhelming her.

It wasn't possible to believe! It couldn't be! This was some crazy dream.

Peter Schmidt saying he loved her, telling her he wanted her?

Suddenly the man was holding her, crushing her

form against his. Krista didn't think or question or wonder about the unreality of it. All that mattered was that Peter had said he loved her.

Peter Schmidt had proclaimed his love.

Their lips met, tenderly, then passionately. After a long while Peter looked down into her eyes. Love filled every feature of his face.

She wanted to believe; but he had fooled her before with his lovely lines and his polished ways. What did he really want? What was he really after?

If only she could believe.

"Think you could put up with a rich man for a husband?" he asked, his voice husky. "A man who has been a bachelor for too many years? Search out that paradise which our love can make for us? Could you ever love such a man? I know it's rather quick—but I make snap decisions!" His voice was filled with emotion.

Krista gazed lovingly up into her man's eyes. There was no need for verbal acceptance, for her eyes said it all. Yet she affirmed it with her lips: "It might be pretty hard, but I could manage it—with a lot of effort!"

She wanted to say more, but their lips met and their bodies fused in an embrace which said it all to both of them in one moment of eternity.

About the Author

Charles Nuetzel was born in San Francisco in 1934, and writes:

"As long as I can remember I wanted to be a writer. It was a dream I never thought would materialize. But with the help of Forrest J Ackerman, who became my agent, I managed to finally make it into print.

"I was lucky enough not only in selling my work to publishers but also ending up packaging books for some of them, and finally becoming a 'publisher' much like those who had bought my first novels. From there it as a simple leap to editing not only a science-fiction anthology, but also a line of SF books for Powell Sci-Fi back in the 1960s. Throughout these active professional years I had the chance to design some covers and do graphic cover layouts for pocket books & magazines."

Much of his work in covers and graphics are a result of having had a father who was a professional commercial artist, and who did a number of covers for sci-fi magazines in the 1950s and later for pocket books—even for some of Mr. Nuetzel's books.

In retirement he has become involved in swing dancing, a long time lover of Big Band jazz. But more interestingly world travels have taken him (and his wife Brigitte) across the world, to Hawaii, Caribbean, Mexico, Kenya, Egypt, Peru, having a lifelong interest in ancient civilizations. His website is full of thousands of pictures taken during these trips.

www.ingramcontent.com/pod-product-compliance
Lightning Source LLC
Chambersburg PA
CBHW030507260626
47157CB00005B/1687